The Mystery
of the Missing Map

Also by Lois Walfrid Johnson

Adventures of the Northwoods

The Riverboat Adventures

Let's-Talk-About-It Stories for Kids

Viking Quest Series

For girls:

The Mystery
of the Missing Map

by

Lois Walfrid Johnson

**MOTT
MEDIA**

Fenton, Michigan

Except for the band director, John Philip Sousa, the characters in this book are fictitious and spring with gratitude for life from the author's imagination. Any resemblance to persons living or dead is coincidental.

Published by Mott Media®
Printed in the United States of America

For information about other Mott Media publications visit our website at www.mottmedia.com.

Cover Artist: Tim Holden

Published in association with the literary agency of Alive Communications, Inc., 7680 Goddard Street, Suite 200, Colorado Springs, CO 80920.

Library of Congress Cataloging-in-Publication Data

Johnson, Lois Walfrid.
    Mystery of the missing map / by Lois Walfrid Johnson.
    p. cm. — (Adventures of the northwoods ; 9)
    Summary: When thirteen-year-old Kate, her stepbrother Anders, and their friend Erik go to visit Kate's blind second cousin in Red Jacket, Michigan, in 1907, they decide to try to find a long-lost map that will supposedly lead to a fortune in silver.
    ISBN 978-0-88062-283-7 (alk. paper)
    [1. Mystery and detective stories. 2. Blind—Fiction. 3. People with disabilities—Fiction. 4. Michigan—History—20th century—Fiction.] I. Title.
  PZ7.J63255Mym 2009
  [Fic]—dc22
                                           2008054838

To Justin,
the ultimate gift of 1990!
Thanks for being someone
who knows how to help others

About the Author

Lois Walfrid Johnson loves kids and young people and loves writing stories for them. A trusted friend of families, she is the author of 38 books, 14 updated editions, and hundreds of shorter pieces. Her fiction series include the Adventures of the Northwoods mysteries, the Riverboat Adventures (steamboat, Underground Railroad, and immigrant history), and the Viking Quest series in which her characters travel from Ireland to Norway, Iceland, and Greenland, then sail with Leif Erickson to what is now America.

Lois started writing her first novel when she was $9^1/_2$. Years later, she finished that book as *The Runaway Clown*, eighth novel in the Northwoods series. A frequent speaker and former instructor for *Writer's Digest* School, Lois has taught writing in a wide variety of situations. Readers have written from more than 40 countries to say, "I love your books. I can't put them down."

Lois' husband, Roy, is a gifted teacher and an idea person for her writing. They especially enjoy time with their family and friends, the Northwoods people and places, and readers like you.

See *www.loiswalfridjohnson.com*.

Contents

Copper Country
Michigan's Keweenaw Peninsula
1907

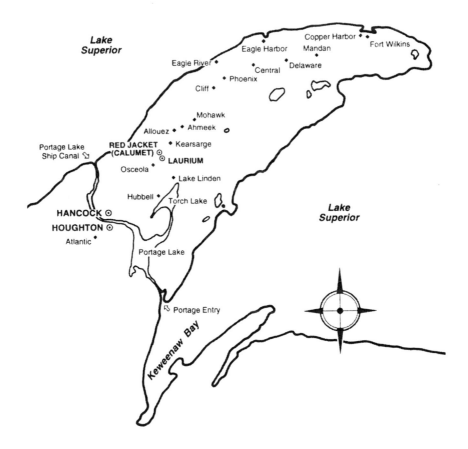

During the time in which Kate, Anders, and Erik visited Michigan's Copper Country, the business district known as Calumet was called Red Jacket. Present-day Calumet and other important sites in the surrounding area are part of the Keweenaw National Historical Park.

The Red Jacket Opera House is now called the Calumet Theatre.

Threats in the Night

A long whistle sounded in the night. Startled, Katherine O'Connell jerked awake. Her eyes flew open as she wondered, *Where am I?*

A dim light pierced the darkness. Beneath Kate, even the floor rumbled.

Again the whistle sounded. Its mournful call helped Kate remember. She was on a train traveling to Michigan's Upper Peninsula. *Soon I'll be in Copper Country! I'll meet my Irish cousin, Megan!*

Even the thought brought Kate more fully awake. In the seat facing hers, Kate's stepbrother Anders was still sleeping. So was their friend Erik Lundgren.

Slowly Kate stood up and stepped around her brother's big feet to reach the aisle. As Kate started through the railroad car, a man glanced up, staring at her with resentful eyes.

Kate shivered and looked away. Just as quickly she glanced back. She had never seen the man before. Why should he act as if he disliked her? Whoever the man was, he had already pulled a hat down over his face.

When Kate reached the rear of the car, she took a long drink at the water cooler. During the night, the gas lights had been turned down, leaving long shadows.

I'll wash up now, Kate thought. In that third week of July 1907, black clouds of smoke often blew in through the open windows. All through the long, hot trip from northwest Wisconsin, soot and cinders had found their way onto Kate's clothing.

The water felt good against her face. When she came out of the washroom, she took another drink. From somewhere she heard voices.

Curious as always, Kate followed the dimly lighted hallway outside the washroom. Beyond a partly open door, two people stood on the platform at the end of the car.

"I tell you, they'll cause trouble," a man said.

"A bunch of brats?" The second voice was low, yet scornful. With the rumble of the train, Kate could barely hear. "How can they upset our plans?"

"I saw them, and they're not stupid. The boys are over six feet tall."

Six feet tall? Kate thought. Whoever the person was, he had to be talking about Anders and Erik. In the land of Swedish-Americans where they lived, that height wasn't unusual for thirteen-year-olds. But now someone had noticed it.

Kate edged forward, as close to the door as she dared. Both people wore men's business suits and hats. With their backs toward Kate, they stood next to the railing that surrounded the platform.

"I heard them talking," the man went on. "The boys look strong. Good muscles in their shoulders. They're used to working."

The other person laughed. "Not like you, huh? What are you, Curly—a coward?"

Again Kate crept forward. Above the clickety-clack of the wheels, she could barely hear the second voice.

"You said it was a quick find, an easy steal," answered the man named Curly. "Already you've been there six months. When are you going to find something?"

"It takes time." The other voice was still muffled by the sounds of the train. "I'll find that map yet."

"I'm tired of working for peanuts!" Curly's voice rose in anger. "Let's get out while we still can."

"No!" The word was sharp and angry.

Kate jumped back. Just in time she remembered the dim light behind her. If the people who were talking turned around, they would see her.

"I'm not giving up now," the second voice went on. "Just do what I tell you!"

Curly's hoarse laugh cut off the rest of the words. "You're not my boss!"

The other voice broke in again. "It all fits—the O'Connells and the Mitchells together."

Kate's stomach tightened. Her cousin Megan's father worked for a man named James Mitchell.

"It's too dangerous," Curly warned.

"Hush, you fool!"

"Don't call *me* a fool!" Curly exclaimed.

"We're wasting time when we need to plan," the other voice answered. "Once we get there, we can't be seen together."

"Well, do you have any more ideas?" Curly asked. "Good ones, I mean."

"Let's use the brats you're so afraid of."

A band of fear tightened around Kate's heart. The person had to mean Anders and Erik and probably her.

"Maybe they'll find something we haven't. Let *them* solve the mystery. Let them lead us to the treasure!"

The treasure? Without thought of her own danger, Kate crept forward again, straining to hear.

"They probably don't even know about it," Curly answered.

"They will," the second voice said. "Everyone coming into the area hears the story, just like we did."

"All right!" Curly sounded resentful. "One more try. But this time I'll make sure we succeed!"

"Don't come see me unless it's late at night," the other voice said. "If you leave a message, make sure it's in our secret code."

"Sure, sure." It was plain Curly didn't like the orders. His face still turned toward the end of the train, he stepped away from the railing, moving closer to Kate.

Filled with panic, she scrambled into the hallway. When she reached the water cooler, she stopped as though planning to take a drink.

As she carefully looked back, a man's hand reached out, pushing the door to the platform farther open. Turning, Kate hurried up the aisle past the seats filled with sleeping people.

Halfway through the car, Kate glanced around. No one seemed to be following her. Just the same, she felt relieved when she reached Anders and Erik again. Dropping down into her seat, she reached forward and tugged her brother's arm. "Anders! Wake up!"

Her brother groaned.

"Anders!" Kate's whisper sounded hoarse.

As though brushing off a pesky fly, Anders swung his arm, almost hitting Kate's face.

"Anders!" Kate was angry now. "It's important!"

"Shhh!" someone hissed from across the aisle. "We're trying to sleep!"

Desperately, Kate kicked her brother's foot. When Anders still didn't waken, she shook Erik's shoulder. "I need help!" she whispered.

Erik opened his eyes. He straightened, fully awake. "What's the matter?"

As quickly as she could, Kate told him. "You've got to see who those men are!"

Erik reached over, pinched Anders' elbow. Anders yowled in pain.

The man across from them leaned into the aisle. "We are trying to sleep!"

Anders was awake now all right. He glared at Erik.

"Sorry, old buddy!" Erik spoke softly. "Kate's found another mystery. I need your help."

"Aw, Erik, come on. Don't listen to her!"

But Erik stood up. "Stay here in case they saw you," he told Kate. "I'll go check."

"C'mon!" Erik urged as he stepped past Anders' legs. "Stop wasting time!"

Still grumbling, Anders ran his fingers through his blond hair and staggered after Erik. Kate twisted around, watching them. Soon the darkness swallowed up both of the boys.

More than a year before, Kate's widowed mother had married Anders' father, Carl Nordstrom. Kate and her Swedish mother had moved from Minneapolis to Windy Hill Farm in northwest Wisconsin.

Now Kate had a stepsister named Tina, two stepbrothers—Anders and Lars, and a new baby brother. Yet Kate often longed to know more about the Irish side of her family.

Recently Mama had written to Daddy's first cousin, Casey O'Connell. Casey had answered by inviting Kate to the northwoods of Michigan's Upper Peninsula. He had even sent train tickets for three people so she wouldn't have to travel alone.

To Kate it seemed forever before Anders and Erik came back. When they did, Anders was even more upset.

"You know, Kate, you have the wildest imagination of any person I've ever met. There was no one around."

"Well, they were there. They got away while you were arguing."

Anders shook his head. "Crazy girl! You're making things up!"

Kate turned to Erik. "You didn't see anything strange?"

Erik shook his head. "Everyone was in their seats. Anders woke up some of them when he yelled."

"Did you see a man with angry eyes?" Kate asked. "Did he look at you?"

Erik shook his head. "Sorry, Kate."

But Anders was not so kind. "You got me up for nothing!"

"For *nothing!*" Kate blurted out. "I heard someone talking—"

"Shhh!" The man from across the aisle no longer whispered. He was clearly upset.

Kate lowered her voice. "They were talking about *you!* You and Erik!"

Anders groaned, slouched down in his seat, and closed his eyes. Kate looked at Erik, hoping he believed her.

Instead, Erik asked, "Kate, are you sure you weren't dreaming? Did you have a nightmare?"

Kate shook her head, so upset that she couldn't answer.

Before long, Erik leaned back against the window. Soon he, too, was asleep.

Kate stared at the boys, unable to believe they could go back to sleep. *Imagination, my eye! I'll show 'em!*

Thinking back, Kate tried to remember every word she'd heard. *How can those people use us to find a treasure?*

Feeling angry and out of sorts, Kate flipped her long braid over her shoulder and stood up. Once again she walked back through the car. The man with the resentful eyes was no longer there.

I'll watch, Kate promised herself as she returned to her seat. *When we reach the village of Red Jacket, I'll notice if there's anything strange.*

But Kate didn't like the uneasy feeling in the pit of her stomach. It had nothing to do with meeting her cousin Megan.

Strange Meeting

The word *treasure* whirled around in Kate's head. *What don't we know? What do we need to find out?*

As the eastern sky grew lighter, Erik woke up. The early-morning sunlight shone on his brown hair. When he saw that Kate was also awake, he leaned forward to talk.

Only a few days before, Kate's family had returned from seeing a circus in River Falls. Kate would never forget how it felt to find Erik on the platform of the Frederic Depot. Countless times she had thought about the way he looked in the moment he saw her.

In the wagon on the way home, everyone had jabbered a mile a minute. Since then, Kate and Erik hadn't been able to talk without someone listening in.

Now Kate glanced at her brother. He was breathing evenly, as though sound asleep. Maybe this was the moment when she could tell Erik how she felt.

"What do you know about your cousin Megan?" Erik spoke in a low voice as if he, too, did not want to wake Anders.

"Not much," Kate admitted. "When Daddy died, Mama and I lost track of Megan's father Casey. All I know is that Megan is my second cousin and about five months younger than I am."

"You haven't even seen a picture?" Erik asked.

Kate shook her head. "I hope we can be best friends."

"You will be, Kate. I'm sure of it!"

"Casey wrote something strange," Kate answered. "He said, 'Please come as soon as you can. Megan wants to meet Kate, and she needs her *now.*' "

"That *is* strange. Why would Megan need you?" Erik asked.

"I don't know. Not even Mama understands. But Casey must really want us to come. It's a lot of money buying tickets for three people."

Erik's grin lit his eyes. "I sure don't mind going with you."

Kate's heart warmed. As often before, she felt grateful to have Erik for a special friend.

Erik lowered his voice, spoke even more softly. "Kate, what happened to you in River Falls?"

Kate swallowed hard. That hadn't been an easy time. Since moving to Windy Hill Farm, she had often been torn between her memories of Michael Reilly and the way she felt about Erik. One part of Kate was scared to tell Erik how she liked him. The other part wanted him to know.

"How did you and Michael get along?" Erik asked.

"Yah, Kate," Anders suddenly broke in. "Tell Erik how you got along."

Erik groaned and made a face. Kate felt the same way. During the night they couldn't wake Anders up. Now he woke up from barely a sound. He had probably listened in on everything they said!

During the morning, the train passed into the Keweenaw Peninsula. Known as the Copper Country because of the great number of copper mines, the Keweenaw was a narrow finger of land at the top of Michigan's Upper Peninsula. Though she could not see Lake Superior, Kate knew that its clear waters surrounded the Keweenaw.

Kate barely saw the beautiful northwoods. More than anything, she wanted to talk to Erik, but she didn't want her brother around. Every time she and Erik had walked to the end of the railroad car, Anders followed.

When the train stopped in Houghton to take on passengers, Kate's thoughts leaped ahead to Megan. For the hundredth time Kate wondered what her cousin would be like.

Soon the train moved on, crossing a long bridge over the Portage Canal. After stopping at Hancock, the locomotive chugged up a steep hill.

Before long, the conductor walked through the car. "Red Jacket next!" he called. "All out for Red Jacket!"

As the locomotive slowed down, Kate leaned out of the window. She wanted the very first glimpse of her newly found cousin. What fun they'd have together!

Cars clanked as the train squealed to a stop. The Mineral Range Depot was full of men and women waiting to meet passengers or collect freight. Seeing them, Kate's heart sank. How would she ever recognize Casey?

"You'll know him," Mama had said. "I saw Casey only once, but he looks like your daddy."

Just the same, finding Casey seemed impossible. To make matters worse, he would have no idea what Kate looked like.

When she stepped down from the train, a tall man stood in Kate's way. She stopped, then circled around. Behind Kate, Erik carried his suitcase and hers. Anders followed with his own luggage.

More people blocked Kate's view. Because of her short height it seemed that everyone else was a giant.

Finally she saw a man with the black hair of the dark Irish. Walking quickly, Kate set off in that direction. As she passed a cluster of people, she looked around for Anders and Erik.

In that instant Kate crashed into someone. All of her frustration spilled out. "Hey! Watch where you're going!"

"Why don't you watch where *you're* going?" The boy's brown eyes seemed to shoot sparks at Kate. His dark brown hair stood on end, making him look like an angry dog.

"I was standing still," he went on. "Are you blind or something?"

"Of course I'm not blind!" Kate sputtered. "Who do you think you are, anyway?"

The boy drew himself up, raised his chin. "I am William Henry Pascoe!"

Kate stepped back. "Well, William Henry Pascoe, I'm trying to find a man named Casey O'Connell."

"So you're the one we're looking for! Casey sent me to pick you up."

"Pick me up?"

"Yup. The boss had an important meeting today. Casey had to drive some big shots around."

William Henry seemed about thirteen years old. Yet he acted as if he always called Casey by his first name. Kate doubted if William Henry talked that way to Casey's face.

"I'm supposed to take you to Megan's," he said now.

"That so?" Kate's voice matched his. Unsure whether she wanted to go with him, Kate turned. "My brother, Anders Nordstrom. Our friend, Erik Lundgren," she said stiffly.

Both Erik and Anders stood a good six inches above the other boy. As he stared up at them, William Henry seemed uneasy.

Just then a girl stepped out from behind him. "Aw, Willie, stop putting on airs!"

The girl's long black hair was braided in two pigtails. Willie tipped his head her way. "This is Megan."

"Hi, Kate," Megan said softly.

As she stared at her cousin, Kate felt as if she were looking in a mirror. Megan had the same black hair and slender body. Even their faces were remarkably similar. Except for a small raised spot, a scar on the bridge of Megan's nose, they looked more alike than most sisters.

"We're twins!" Kate blurted out.

"We are?" Megan sounded surprised.

Kate laughed. "Can't you see it? If we wore the same clothes, no one could tell us apart."

Megan smiled, but her gaze did not meet Kate's.

"Look at me!" Kate answered, still filled with the fun of it. "Same black hair, same mouth, same—"

Suddenly she broke off. *Same eyes*, she was about to say. But in that moment Megan looked directly at Kate.

Like Kate's eyes, Megan's were deep blue, but the pupils were larger. Those large black pupils looked at Kate as though they did not focus.

Kate caught her breath. Before she could think, an "Oh!" escaped her lips. She clapped a hand over her mouth.

But Megan caught the sound. "Didn't you know that I'm blind?"

Kate shook her head, then remembered that Megan couldn't see her. "No," Kate said weakly. "No one told me."

Inside, Kate wanted to cry out against those people. *I could have asked Mama what to do!*

Kate struggled to speak. "I'm sorry that you're blind."

"I'm sorry too," Megan said. She looked tired, as though she'd been through this a thousand times.

Kate stumbled for something to say. "We'll still have fun together."

"We'll see," Megan answered. She sounded like a grown-up, unwilling to make a promise to a small child.

Kate guessed that Megan didn't believe her. *Well, I'll make sure we have fun*, Kate thought.

"Come on," Willie said to Anders and Erik. "I'll take you to Megan's."

Willie grabbed Megan's arm, but she shook him off. Instead, she took his arm.

"Remember?" she asked, as if he seldom helped her. "You lead me, instead of my walking ahead of you."

Willie set off at a good pace, and Megan kept up. They were partway through the crowd when Willie stopped. "I almost forgot. Casey said I should pick up Tisha."

Tee-sha? Kate thought as she listened to how Willie pronounced it. *That's a new name.*

Willie glanced around, then stood on tiptoe. "Where is she?"

Near the depot, a tall woman stood alone, impatiently tapping one foot.

"There she is!" Willie exclaimed. He started in that direction, and the rest of them followed.

When they reached the woman, Willie explained. "Tisha's just back from a few days off. She's housekeeper for Mitchells."

The woman's blond hair was stiffly curled, with every strand perfectly in place. Tisha nodded at the boys but looked down her nose at Kate. Her cold blue eyes seemed to take in every detail of Kate's grimy dress. In spite of the soot from the train, Tisha looked as clean as if she had just washed her clothes.

"Let's get started, Willie," Tisha said, handing him her suitcase. It was more a command than a request.

She's pretty, Kate thought. *But she sure doesn't act pretty.*

Megan took Willie's free hand, and Tisha led all of them toward a hitching rail. Holding her head proudly, she walked straight up to a pair of matched grays. The spirited horses stood in front of a three-seated buggy with leather upholstered seats.

Tisha waited for Willie to give her a hand into the buggy. Sitting down in the last seat, she spread out her full skirt like a queen arranging herself on a throne.

Willie helped Megan into the buggy, and Kate climbed up next to her. Anders dropped down on the front seat. That meant Erik had no choice but to sit with Tisha. Most of the seat was filled by the woman's skirt.

Erik hesitated. "May I sit here?" he asked politely.

Tisha looked as though she didn't want to share the seat, but finally moved her skirt.

Willie strapped the suitcases to the end of the buggy, walked around to the front, and leaped up to the high seat. As he sat down, he clucked to the horses, and they backed away from the rail.

Soon Willie drove the buggy past the twin steeples of a large building. A sign told Kate it was St. Joseph's Catholic Church under construction. Workmen were putting in great stained-glass windows.

"Oh, look!" Kate said to Megan. Then she remembered. Megan

couldn't see the beautiful colors. Embarrassed, Kate tried to think what she could say. Yet she couldn't get past the awfulness of Willie's words at the depot.

"Are you blind or something?" he had asked Kate. No wonder Megan acted as if she didn't like him.

Kate's own words bothered her even more. She wanted to crawl into a snail's shell and stay there.

"Nice looking grays," Anders said as Willie made a right turn.

"Fastest horses around," Willie boasted.

A moment later Megan leaned forward. "Willie, you're going the wrong way."

"Giving 'em a tour of the town!" Willie didn't like being found out.

"Daddy said you're supposed to go straight home—that Kate would be tired of riding."

Megan turned back to Kate. "My father is the grounds keeper and chauffeur for Mr. Mitchell. Willie's the stableboy."

Anders grinned at Willie. "In other words, you muck out after the horses."

Willie flushed.

But Anders kept his face as serious as if he never did the same work. "Would I have to know someone important to get a job like that?" he asked.

His hands still on the reins, Willie looked back at Megan. An angry light filled his eyes. "I'm gonna find me that treasure and bust out of here."

"Sure," Megan said. "You're going to find the treasure just like I'm going to find my sight. Daddy said that if you don't obey, you won't get to take the buggy again."

Willie shrugged. Just the same, he turned the horses at the next corner. The cedar blocks on which they rode changed to concrete. The horses clip-clopped along on the hard surface.

Up till now, Kate had never seen a concrete street. She liked the rhythm made by the horses' hooves. *Is that how Megan knew what Willie was doing?* Kate wondered. *Through the sounds made by different kinds of roads?*

"My parents are sorry they couldn't meet you," Megan said now. "Ma cooks for the Mitchells. She's making lunch for the men who are in town."

"What did Willie mean by a treasure?" Kate asked.

"Oh, Willie's crazy!" Megan brushed the question off.

Two blocks farther on, Willie directed the horses left. Again he looked back at Megan. "All right if I show them the sights?"

"If they're on the way," she answered stiffly.

Soon they rode past a large brick and sandstone building with a tall steeple. "Red Jacket Town Hall and Opera House," Willie told them, as though he were a tour guide.

"All kinds of famous actors and actresses have come here," Megan said to Kate. "The band director John Philip Sousa has been here twice."

At the corner Willie turned onto Elm. A block later he turned again onto a narrow street filled with horses and wagons.

Tall buildings rose above the cement sidewalks. On a lower light brick building, Kate noticed the words:

PAINE WEBBER
AND
COMPANY
BOSTON, MASS.

In the street ahead, an ice wagon slowed down and pulled over. Then an automobile tried to get through. From behind their buggy, Kate heard a clunk.

"Willie!" Megan spoke sharply. "You dropped a suitcase!"

As he turned around, Willie looked weary of Megan's instructions. In the next moment his expression changed. He tugged sharply on the reins.

Kate looked back. "Oh no!" An open suitcase lay in the middle of the street. "It's mine!"

Her good white dress and underclothes had spilled out, right in the path of an oncoming horse.

3

Cousin Casey

The horse's front hoof tromped down on Kate's white dress. An instant later, a back hoof landed on the suitcase and kicked it aside. A wheel caught Kate's best skirt, dragging it across the rough pavement.

Kate moaned. The minute Willie stopped the buggy, she jumped down.

"Kate!" Erik yelled as another horse bore down upon her.

Kate looked up, gulped, but could not move. Just in time the horse sidestepped Kate. Large wagon wheels rumbled past, less than a foot from where she stood.

Erik leaped down, pulled Kate onto the sidewalk. "I can't believe you did that! Right in the path of a wagon!"

In all the time Kate had known him, she'd never seen Erik so upset. "Phooey!" she answered. "I had plenty of room!"

"You did not! You could have been killed. All for one stupid suitcase!"

Then Kate remembered. "My clothes!"

With angry steps, she hurried back in the direction from which they had come. Erik caught Kate's arm to keep her on the sidewalk.

As they reached the suitcase, a big draft horse stepped around it. A moment later, the heavy wagon rolled over the suitcase, crushing it flat. The wheel left a black line across Kate's dress.

Kate groaned. "My good white dress!"

More than a block away, a carriage moved toward them, and Kate saw her chance. Running out into the street, she snatched up her dress and stuffed her underclothes into the wrecked suitcase.

Erik took the suitcase from her. Holding it carefully, he carried it back to the sidewalk.

Willie met them there. He had pulled the buggy off to one side.

"Thanks a lot!" Kate told him.

"Don't mention it."

His careless remark made things even worse. *"Don't mention it!"* Kate exclaimed. "I'll mention it as much as I want, for the whole time I have to see your ugly face. Look at that suitcase! It's your fault!"

"No damage done!" Willie grabbed the handle, taking Erik by surprise. Just then the broken hinges let go. All of Kate's clothes spilled out again.

Kate's whole being flooded with anger. "I haven't got words to describe you!"

More embarrassed than ever, she knelt down on the sidewalk, snatched up her underclothes again, and stuffed them into what remained of the suitcase.

Standing up, Kate clutched the entire mess. This time she allowed no one to take it from her. Her chin high, Kate stalked back to the buggy.

The boys followed. As the three of them climbed into the buggy, not even Willie dared speak a word.

Farther down the street, Kate saw her best skirt, where it had been dragged by the passing wagon. This time Erik jumped down, picked it up, and handed it to Kate.

When they turned onto Red Jacket Road, Kate glanced back at Tisha. As if suitcases fell apart on the street every day, she looked calmly ahead. Her cool expression angered Kate even more. *Tee-sha*, she thought, remembering how Willie said the housekeeper's name. *I do not like you!*

When Kate could finally speak she muttered in Megan's ear. "I've never been so embarrassed in all my life!"

Her cousin reached out, found Kate's hand and squeezed it. "I'm sorry. Are your clothes wrecked?"

Kate sighed. "I don't know if I'll ever get them clean again. And some are torn."

"Well, I won't know the difference," Megan answered.

Kate giggled. "Did you mean that to be funny?"

Megan's lips quivered, as though she wanted to smile. She seemed surprised that Kate had laughed. "I guess I was trying to make you feel better. Are we the same size? You can wear my clothes."

"Thanks, Megan." Kate did feel better.

Just then a loud whistle split the air. Kate jumped at the unexpected noise. It sounded as if a locomotive was close by.

"It's the C & H whistle," Megan told her. "We tell time by their whistles. That's the one for lunch."

"What's C & H?" Kate asked.

Willie swung around, answering for Megan. "Calumet and Hecla. The richest copper mine on earth."

"Willie, keep your eyes on the road," Megan told him.

Willie glared at her. "These horses are not going to run into anything!"

Kate was glad Megan couldn't see Willie's expression. To Kate's relief he turned and faced forward. The busy streets were a noisy contrast to the quiet of Windy Hill Farm.

"We're leaving Red Jacket and going into Laurium," Megan said soon. "The two villages are next to each other. People of every nationality live in our area."

Kate knew Megan was trying to smooth things over. But Kate still felt on edge—not only about her clothes, but also because of what had happened at the depot. Again Kate wondered how Megan felt about the way Willie treated her. *Is that what Casey meant when he said that Megan needs me?*

Behind Kate, Erik was silent, as though he had given up trying to talk with Tisha. Now he leaned forward.

"How long have you been blind?" Erik asked Megan. His voice sounded as natural as if he wanted to know what she had for breakfast. Kate felt grateful.

"Almost three years," Megan said, as if she answered the question every day. "I stood up in a wagon before it stopped completely. I fell out and hit my head on a rock. Landed right here."

She touched the small scar between her eyes. "I broke my nose and the little bones between my eyes. When I woke up from a coma, I couldn't see."

"Not at all?" Erik asked. "Do you know whether it's night or day?"

"I see a little crack of light here, way off to the side." Megan held her hand back above her right shoulder. "That's how I know if it's light or dark. But if I turn my eyes and try to look at it, the crack of light is farther off to the right."

Kate couldn't imagine what it would be like to be blind. Right then and there she promised herself she'd do everything she could to help Megan.

As the horses entered a street lined with mansions, Megan spoke again. "Do we really truly look alike?"

"Very much alike," Kate answered.

Megan smiled. "I always wanted a sister."

"So did I," Kate said. "I have one now, but Tina's much younger than I am."

Kate pulled her long braid forward. "You wear your hair different from mine." She tipped her head and guided Megan's hand so she could feel. "If I wore your clothes and braided my hair like yours—"

Megan shook her head. "You can wear my clothes, but I'll braid my hair like *yours*!"

Kate grinned. She was liking this cousin of hers more all the time.

"Then we'll look alike?" Megan asked.

"People who don't know us won't be able to tell us apart," Kate said.

Anders turned around. "Just one thing. I sure hope you don't get into as much trouble as Kate!"

When they came to a mansion with a porch across the front and around both sides, Willie turned the horses into the driveway. Large pillars supported the roof over the part of the driveway next to a side entrance. There Willie stopped the horses.

Picking up her skirts like a great lady, Tisha stepped out on a cement carriage block, then onto the porch.

Willie pulled around to the stable at the back of the mansion and stopped again. Putting her foot on the step between the two wheels, Kate hopped down. Remembering Megan, she turned back to help.

"It's a big step," Kate warned.

Megan found the step between the wheels with her foot, then dropped down as lightly as Kate. "I know it's a big step," Megan told her. "I do it all the time."

She started walking toward a two-story building beyond the stable. "We live in the carriage house," she explained to Kate.

Already Willie was backing the buggy into the bottom half of the building. A flight of steps led up the outside to the second floor.

Megan led them toward the stairs, while Willie unhitched the horses.

"Careful!" Kate warned as Megan reached them. "There are steps in front of you."

Megan whirled around. "I know there are steps," she said. "I live here."

Megan's voice sounded strained, as if she was trying to be polite. Stretching out her hand, she found the railing and started up.

Kate bit her tongue, wishing she could take back her words. Only a moment ago, she had felt close to Megan. Now everything had changed again.

Kate felt miserable. Clutching her clothes and broken suitcase, she followed her cousin.

At the top of the stairs was a landing. A door led into the apartment where Megan's family lived. Just inside, the wonderful smell of cooking filled the eating area and small kitchen.

Kate breathed deeply. "Mmmm!" She looked forward to Cousin Breda's good food.

"Ma will soon be home from making lunch at the Mitchell's," Megan explained as she led Kate on.

Beyond the kitchen, a small sitting room overlooked a large flower garden. Two bedrooms lay off the sitting room—one for Megan's parents, the other for Megan.

Megan led Kate into her room. Though pushed against the outside wall, a double bed filled most of the room. Only a two-foot-wide space separated the bed from a dresser and small desk. Another three-foot space at the end of the bed gave enough room for the door to open.

"If you think it looks like a closet, that's what it was!" Megan said lightly. "Daddy fixed it so I could have my own room."

Kate dropped her dirty clothes in the narrow space between the end of the bed and the door.

"Where are they?" Megan asked quickly.

"My clothes? On the floor."

Suddenly it dawned on Kate what was wrong. If she left them there, Megan might trip. Kate leaned down, snatched up her clothes, and stuffed them under the bed.

"I made a place for you," Megan said. Behind the door were three pegs for clothing. Two of the pegs were empty. "When your clothes are clean again, why don't you hang them here?"

Moving quickly as if she knew every step, Megan led Kate back to the kitchen. Along one wall was a wood cookstove, much like the one at Windy Hill Farm. Megan pulled a big kettle forward to the warmest part of the stove.

"I made Irish stew before we went to the depot," Megan said.

"You made it?" Kate was surprised. "Not your mom?"

"I'm a good cook," Megan answered stiffly. "Don't you know how to cook?"

"Well, sure, but . . . " Kate paused, embarrassed again.

"Just because I'm blind doesn't mean I can't do anything!" Megan turned toward the stove. "As soon as we dish up, we're ready to eat."

The table was already set, and Kate had no doubt about who had done that. In the center of the table was a small vase filled with flowers.

After eating out of a picnic basket the entire trip, Kate looked forward to a real meal. When the boys came in, they all sat down.

Bowing her head, Megan prayed quickly. "Thank you, Father. Thank you that Kate and Anders and Erik could come. Thank you for this good food."

As she listened to Megan pray, Kate felt better. In spite of all that had gone wrong, she knew they had an important bond.

They had almost finished eating when a quick step sounded on the stairs outside. A moment later, a man with black wavy hair appeared in the doorway. When he saw Kate and the boys, he spread his arms wide.

"A hundred thousand welcomes!"

Another Fight

Casey's blue eyes danced. He stared at Kate, then declared, "Ah, child, it's the look of the Irish you have!"

"And she looks like me?" Megan asked eagerly.

"Well, now, let's see." Casey pulled both of them to their feet, lined them up side by side. He patted Megan's head, then Kate's.

"One inch difference there. You have to eat more vegetables, Megan. But you both have black hair."

Casey stepped back, still gazing at Kate. "You're an O'Connell, all right. Deep blue eyes. Rosy cheeks. Are you as spunky?"

Anders laughed. "Wait till you know her!"

"Hmmm." Casey winked at Kate. "I'll have to find out what that means."

He swung the girls around, yanked one of Megan's braids, then Kate's long one. "Sure and if both of you haven't got good braids for pulling!"

Megan squealed, and Casey caught her hands. "Let's see how you are with an Irish jig."

He swung Megan around the table, narrowly missing a bookcase along the wall. Megan followed him, as light on her feet as if she saw every step of the way.

He's like Daddy! Kate thought. The two men had the same build and the same color hair, except that Casey's was dusted with gray. But their laughs were the most similar—their laughs and the way Casey danced.

In all the time since Daddy O'Connell had died, Kate had held a memory close to her heart. When Daddy came home from work, he always swung her off her feet with a big hug. Then he'd dance around the kitchen, leading her in an Irish jig.

Without warning, sudden tears blurred Kate's vision. A lonely ache tightened her chest. She blinked, brushed the tears away and tried to pretend nothing had happened.

Just then Casey stopped in front of her. His blue eyes twinkled with fun as he bowed low. "Well, now, let's see if you can keep up with me."

He took Kate's hand, then remembered. "Ah! We forgot the music!"

Quickly he cranked a handle on the side of a wooden box. He put on a record, then set the arm with its needle in place. Music filled the room.

Once more, Casey bowed in front of Kate. "May I have the honor?"

By now Kate could smile and step off in a lively jig. Casey twirled her around the table, then past a chair, into the small sitting room and back. His feet moved lightly, faster and faster. Kate followed, feeling as if it was only yesterday since she whirled around the kitchen with Daddy.

Finally Casey stopped, breathless and laughing. "Whoa, whoa, whoa! You've got a bit of the Irish, all right. Guess you'll pass as an O'Connell."

He drew a deep breath. "You've learned to dance somewhere. Your daddy teach you?"

Kate nodded, afraid to speak. Even looking at Casey made her lonesome for her father.

For a moment Casey studied Kate's face. As if guessing that Daddy's memory still brought pain, he spoke softly. "Sometimes cousins look more alike than sisters or brothers."

As though knowing she couldn't talk just then, Casey looked away. "Well, Megan, me girl," he said. "You're almost the same height, you have the same black hair, and you're both good dancers. What else do you want to know?"

"Our faces. They're really alike?"

"You're both as lovely as the Rose of Tralee," Casey answered. "We'll have to find out if there are ways you're different."

"That won't be hard!" Anders exclaimed. "What about you, Megan? Do you have a temper?"

Megan shook her head, but Casey's laugh gave her away.

"Are you as curious as a cat?" Erik asked.

A quick shadow passed over Megan's face. She nodded, but in the next instant shook her head.

She's curious, all right, Kate thought. *But what happens if you're curious and blind? If you can no longer see all the things you long to see?* Kate felt awkward, almost guilty that she could see and Megan couldn't.

"We better study this situation," Casey said. "Who can we fool into wondering which girl is which?"

Just then the outside door opened. Her long dress covered by a white apron, Cousin Breda stood in the doorway. She looked from one person to the next, then back to Kate.

"Megan, me darlin'," she said. "It's plain as the nose on your face that you have a twin."

Megan's laugh sounded like a silvery bell. She extended her hand in the direction from which Anders had spoken. "Kate's stepbrother Anders came with her. And this is their friend Erik." Again she stretched out her hand, this time toward Erik.

A smile lit Cousin Breda's round face. "It's welcome, you are! And did you get enough to eat?"

Kate laughed. "Don't give the boys any more, or they'll eat you out of house and home."

"Ah, we won't worry about that! It's always easy to cut a potato in half."

When it came time to clean up the kitchen, Megan again took the lead. As she washed the dishes, her sensitive fingers felt each plate before she passed it to Kate for rinsing. Always the plates were clean.

Cousin Breda stopped them. "Thank you, thank you, but I can tidy up here. Run along with you now. Megan, why don't you show Kate around?"

The boys had already vanished. Megan dried her hands and turned to Kate. "Are you ready to go?"

Kate nodded, then remembered to answer yes. "If I know Anders and Erik, they'll be in the stable, looking at horses."

"They both like horses?" Megan asked.

"So do I," Kate answered. "Anders has a horse named Wildfire. Sometimes he lets me ride her. It's so much fun, I wish I had a horse of my own."

Kate followed Megan down the steps outside the carriage house. "Do you like horses?" Kate asked as they walked on.

Suddenly she stopped, once again embarrassed. *Here I am, wanting a horse, and that's what hurt Megan—a horse that moved at the wrong time.*

"I always put my foot in my mouth," Kate said quickly. "Do you hate horses now because of your accident?"

"It wasn't the horse's fault." Megan answered as though she had thought it all through. "I was the one who stood up when I shouldn't have."

As Kate had guessed, they found the boys in one of the stalls, looking at a horse. In the July heat the barn was warm and stuffy. Only a breeze through an open window made it bearable. Returning to the door, Kate propped it half open to catch the cooler air.

"Is your pa going to the Central Mine reunion?" Megan asked Willie.

Willie was sitting on an overturned bucket. He shook his head.

Megan repeated the question. "Is he going to the reunion tomorrow?"

"No, I said." Willie sounded impatient.

"I didn't hear you."

"Well, listen," he growled. Kate felt sure Willie had deliberately misled Megan.

"Pa can't go," Willie went on. "I'm going alone."

"Can we go with you?" Megan asked quickly. "My parents can't go either."

"Who's we?" Willie sounded as sour as a dill pickle.

"Kate and Anders and Erik and me. It'd be fun for them."

Willie groaned. "I don't want to take a whole convention along. I'm going to see my friends."

"Well, make some new friends!" Megan answered impatiently.

"Can't find any better than the ones I've got."

"Just let us go with you on the train." Megan sounded as if she was trying hard to be nice. "It's not the depot where Kate came in. I don't know how to get there. When we get to Central, you can find your old friends."

"What's at Central Mine?" Kate asked.

Megan turned toward her. "Willie's pa used to work there. So did Daddy—for five years after he came to America. When the mine closed in 1898, people scattered all over. The first reunion is tomorrow."

"We'd get to see a mine?" Kate asked quickly.

"Don't bet on it!" Willie still sounded sour.

"Ah, c'mon, Willie," Megan answered.

"I said no, and I mean it!"

Megan spun around, the expression on her face a mixture of hopelessness and hurt. Angrily she stalked away. An instant later she crashed into the half-open door.

"Ow, ow, ow!" Megan cried out. Her hands flew up and covered her face.

Kate flew to her side. "Oh, Megan!"

Megan whirled on her, more upset than ever. "What did you *do*?"

A bright red welt was already rising on the side of her face. The angry line of red extended from her temple past her eyebrow down into her cheekbone.

Kate swallowed hard. "I propped open the door. It was hot—"

"Don't you ever do that again!" Megan exclaimed. "Don't you know it's one of the worst things you can do to me?"

Suddenly she began to weep. Just as suddenly she stopped, as if ashamed to have anyone see her cry. "Either leave a door all the way open or all the way shut!"

Megan's voice trembled. Reaching out, she felt around until one hand touched the edge of the door. Her other hand extended, Megan passed through the doorway. Once outside, she hurried toward the carriage house.

Kate ran after her. "Megan, I'm sorry!"

Megan seemed not to hear. Her hands still extended as if she were now unsure of everything, she reached the steps. Grasping the railing, she started up. Halfway, she stopped and looked down. "Kate, I can't stand the way you treat me!"

Startled, Kate stared up at her. "What do you mean?"

"Like I'm a baby. Like I don't know what I'm doing. Between you and Willie—"

"Willie?" Kate had noticed how he acted all right. Always he and Megan seemed on the edge of a fight, like a kettle of water ready to boil over.

"It's like he tries to think up things to make me miserable!"

Turning, Megan hurried on, climbing the steps as though she didn't care if she fell to the ground far below.

5

Weird Shadows

Kate whirled around. She couldn't remember when she had been so upset. Reaching the stable, she hurried inside.

"Just who do you think you are, William Henry Pascoe?"

Willie stood up, as though wanting to be on his feet to meet whatever she said. "So try to put the blame on me. It was your fault, and you know it!"

"Yes, it was my fault," Kate admitted. "And I'll try not to leave a door half open. But you were an absolute stinker!"

Willie laughed sharply.

Kate was only warming up. "How can you be so—so—"

Willie raised his chin as though ready to fight.

Kate glared at him. "We are going with you tomorrow. We're going because we don't know how to get there otherwise. But when we reach Central, I hope with all my heart that you disappear!"

"Well, that won't be hard!"

"And we'll find our own way home again!"

"Good!"

"Then that's settled." Kate stalked out of the barn.

Willie called after her. "I'm not going to make it fun for any of you!"

Kate whirled around. It didn't matter that she was thirteen years old. She stuck out her tongue.

When she reached the steps of the carriage house, she took them two at a time. She found Cousin Breda and Cousin Casey sitting at the kitchen table.

All of Kate's anger spilled out. "Why didn't you tell me?" she asked. "Why didn't you tell us that Megan is blind? All the way here I planned the fun we would have!"

Kate broke off, ashamed of herself. *I feel sorry for myself when Megan can't see?* Yet it bothered her. "Everything I do is wrong!"

Casey's eyebrows shot up. "You didn't know?"

Kate shook her head, the pain of it like a hot coal burning her insides.

"When I heard about Brendan—your daddy—dying, I wrote your ma," Casey answered. "I told her how sorry I was about losing such a grand fellow. And I told her about Megan."

"We never got the letter," Kate said.

"You're sure?"

"I would have remembered."

"I wondered why your ma didn't answer," Casey said. "I thought she was too upset about your daddy's death."

In that instant Kate's anger fell apart. She thought back, then understood.

"After Daddy died, Mama and I moved to a smaller apartment." Kate remembered those months when it was hard to pay the rent. "Somewhere the letter must have been lost."

"We should have written before that," Breda said. "We didn't want to believe Megan was really blind. We kept praying that she would get better, that the good Lord would give us a miracle. But as the days wore on—"

"Megan's injury caused swelling in her brain," Casey explained. "She fell unconscious and went into a coma. We were so afraid she would die."

Tears welled up in Casey's eyes just talking about it. "On the fifth day Megan finally woke up. The thin sinus bones behind the bridge of her nose had damaged her optic nerve. That's why she's blind."

"But we still have our precious girl," Breda said.

Casey stood up. "Well, I better get back to work." His steps sounded heavy as he went down the outside stairway.

"Why do Megan and Willie fight so much?" Kate asked.

Breda shrugged. "There's an old Irish saying, 'Better the fighting than the loneliness.' Sometimes people fight just to get attention."

Sunlight through a window added a touch of gold to Breda's red hair. "You know, Kate, God doesn't always make everything go the way we want."

She leaned forward as though wanting to be sure Kate understood. "But God helps us live with things. When you know Megan, you'll find that she sees better than most of us."

Just then the bedroom door opened, and Megan came out. As she walked over to the water pail, she held her head high. Filling the dipper, she took a long drink.

"Willie said we can go to the reunion together," Kate told her.

Megan turned toward the sound of Kate's voice. Her eyes were red and swollen from crying. "What did you do to make him say yes?" The welt on her face stood out.

"Megan, me darlin'!" Breda wailed. "What did you do to your face?"

A knife twisted in Kate's stomach. "I left a door half open," she said.

Breda jumped up. "Let me get some ice."

Megan brushed her mother off. "I can do it myself."

"But you won't."

"I'm going to make a cake for the picnic."

"A cake?" Kate asked quickly. "I can do it."

"So can I," Megan answered shortly, and Kate knew she had again said the wrong thing.

Megan opened a cupboard door and took down a bowl. With a good deal of noisy rattling around, she opened a drawer for measuring cups and spoons. "I'll show that Willie Pascoe I'm not as helpless as he thinks!"

From a shelf, Megan took down a wooden box, set it on the table, and lifted off the cover. The box was filled with pieces of thick paper. Megan pulled out the first piece and laid it on the table.

The paper was filled with raised dots. Megan ran the tips of her fingers across them.

"Cornish Heavy Cake," she read aloud. "I'll prove what a good cook I am! I'll make the cake that Willie likes best!"

Kate stared down at Megan's recipe. "What's that?" she asked.

"Braille symbols. Haven't you seen them before?"

Megan turned the paper so that Kate could have a better look. "Ma read the recipe, and I copied it down."

"But how do you make the dots?" Kate asked.

Megan showed Kate a metal slate with two halves that opened like a book. The bottom half was filled with rows of indented dots, set in groups of six. The top half had small holes opening over the dots.

Megan put a piece of thick paper over the bottom part of the slate, closed the top half, and picked up what she called a stylus.

The small tool had a short handle and what looked like a nail with a rounded end. Working rapidly, Megan punched dots on the right side of the paper, moving left.

When she finished, Megan took out the paper and turned it over. On this side the indented dots had become raised dots. "Now I read from left to right, just like you do," she explained. "I wrote your name."

As Megan began measuring sugar, flour, and salt from pottery crocks, Kate heated water to wash her clothes. Her white dress looked so awful it seemed impossible to wash, dry, mend, and iron it for the next day.

"I'll have to wear something else," Kate said finally.

"Try the green dress in my room," Megan answered.

"How do you know the dress is green?" Kate asked as she returned to the kitchen.

Megan grinned. "Ma told me. I remember by the feel of the cloth. Or if something has a design embroidered on it, that helps me."

Megan left her mixing to show Kate two skirts that were the same except for color. "This one's blue, and this one's black." Inside the waistband, Megan had sewed small *x*'s that told her which color was which.

Back in the kitchen again, Megan rolled out what looked like bread dough.

"That's heavy cake?" Kate asked. "It looks like pastry."

Megan folded the dough, gave it a turn, and folded it again. "It's a Cornish favorite."

Megan laid the dough on a pan and opened the oven door. "It's really rich. Filled with currants and cinnamon and lots of sugar."

Soon the kitchen felt like a steam bath from the heat of the wood cookstove. Yet the wonderful scent of baking also filled the apartment. Moments after Megan set the cake on a cooling rack, Anders and Erik entered the kitchen.

Anders sniffed deeply. "Bet you made that for us."

"Yah, sure!" Megan had already caught on to the way Anders talked. "But you can't eat it till tomorrow."

No matter how much Anders teased, Megan would not give in.

That evening, when it was time to say good-night, Megan told Kate to take the side of the bed next to the window. "I'm used to a hot room," she said. "You'll get more air there."

Moments after Kate's head hit the pillow, she fell asleep. Some time during the night she suddenly woke up.

What is it? Kate wondered, straining to hear. Some noise had disturbed her sleep, but everything was quiet now.

Sitting up, Kate stared out the window. As her eyes grew used to the darkness, she saw the outline of the flower garden below, then the larger shape of the mansion. An electric light shone from the corner across the street.

No horses clip-clopped by. Every house was dark. It had to be very late. Again Kate wondered why she had wakened. Whatever the reason, she felt uneasy.

Then she caught a movement. Beneath a tree Kate saw two shadows that blended with the overhanging leaves. Yet the streetlight gave the shadows a shape.

Kate leaned forward into the window. The people stood close together, as though talking. One was a man, Kate felt sure—a man of medium to tall height.

The other? It was harder to tell. Whoever it was stood in the deepest shadow, close to the trunk of the tree.

Again Kate tried to hear. Was that a low murmur reaching her ears? Kate couldn't be sure. She only knew that something was wrong.

What are they doing there at this hour? For some strange reason Kate remembered the two people talking on the train.

"Megan?" Kate whispered, wanting her help. But Megan did not answer.

6

The Lost Treasure

"Megan?" Kate whispered again. She poked her cousin, and Megan came awake.

"What's the matter?" Megan asked.

"There are two people outside, creeping around in the shadows."

Megan sat up, moved over next to the window.

"Can you hear them?" Kate asked. "You hear better than I do."

"I don't hear better," Megan whispered. "I just listen more."

She leaned close to the window. Like Kate, she strained to hear. Finally Megan shook her head. "There's no one there now."

Kate stared at the shadows by the tree. Megan was right. The people were gone.

"Whoever it was, they're up to no good!" Kate exclaimed.

Megan moved away from the window, back to her side of the bed. Outside, shadows shifted with the streetlight, but here the room was totally dark.

"I've heard voices there before," Megan said. "I always thought it was a man bringing his girl friend home. Why do you think something's wrong?"

"The way they acted," Kate answered. "The way they stayed in the shadows."

"You're really curious, aren't you?" Megan asked.

"As curious as a cat, Anders says. You said you listen. I notice things."

"What do you notice about me?" Megan asked quietly.

The room was so dark that Kate could not see her cousin's face. Somehow it helped Kate to think of Megan in a new way, to catch a small glimpse of her world.

"I hear a really nice voice," Kate said. "I'd like to hear you sing."

"Well, you'll have a chance," Megan answered. "I'm supposed to sing in a contest while you're here. What else do you notice about me?"

"I see someone who cares about people, even when they hurt you," Kate answered.

"Like Willie?"

"Like Willie. Have you known him long?"

"At Central Mine we lived next door," Megan answered. "After the mine closed, Willie's pa followed us here. Our families have always been friends."

"And you had fun together?" Kate asked.

"When I could still see." Megan fell silent, as if thinking about that time when her world was so different.

"I like to play games," she said finally. "I like to run, to feel the wind in my hair. I used to be a really fast runner, and now I don't do it at all."

The ache within Kate was there again, twisting her insides. The way she had hurt Megan stood like a wall in front of Kate. If she didn't say something, it would always haunt her.

"Megan, I'm really sorry about that door."

"You didn't know," Megan told her. "You didn't mean to hurt me."

"Will you forgive me?" Kate asked.

"I already have," Megan answered.

"And for the way I talked?"

"What do you mean?" Megan sounded puzzled.

"At the depot. The way I said, 'Don't you see? Look at me!' "

"Oh! That's all right, Kate. It's the way we talk. I use the same words."

"But doesn't it hurt?" asked Kate.

"Once it did. Right after the accident when I was mad about every-thing. Now it hurts only if someone is trying to be mean. I see things, too, but I see by touching or hearing or smelling."

Kate wished she could see Megan now, but the darkness was too deep. "Megan," she said. "I just want to be friends. To have fun together. To be real cousins."

"You're different from Willie," Megan answered.

"How?"

"To him I'm a bother. He's impatient with me."

"Maybe you're imagining things," Kate said, though she knew that Megan was probably right.

Megan gave an unladylike snort. "I am *not* imagining things. I can tell by the feel of his arm when he helps me. Or the sound of his voice.

I'm a nuisance to him—someone he has to put up with because he works here."

For a moment Megan was silent, as though afraid to say more. When she finally spoke, her words tumbled out. "Kate, it was terrible losing my sight—to see one day and not be able to see the next. But there's something I think is even worse."

"What's that?" Kate asked.

"When I'm ignored—left out. When other kids don't invite me to do things with them. Even though I'm blind, I'm a person, Kate. Just like everyone else."

Kate reached out, wanting to hug her cousin. Instead, she touched Megan's face. Her cousin's cheek was wet with tears. Gently Kate tried to wipe them away.

But Megan talked on, her earnest voice filling the darkness. "I don't want to sit around feeling sorry for myself. I want to do everything I possibly can!"

This time Kate managed to hug her cousin. Megan hugged Kate as though she would never let her go.

When Kate leaned back against the window again, Megan sniffled, then blew her nose. "Thanks, Kate," she said at last.

"We'll do everything together," Kate promised.

The moment the words left her lips Kate felt scared. *Can I really keep my word? I don't want to disappoint Megan.*

* * * * *

In the morning Megan brushed out her black hair, and Kate found it was almost as long as her own. Megan pulled her hair into one long braid.

While Megan was still dressing, Kate went out to the kitchen. Breda was already cooking breakfast at the mansion. But Kate told Casey about the strangers she had heard during the night.

"I'll keep a sharp eye," he said. Soon he left to talk with Mr. Mitchell.

Anders and Erik had slept on the floor of the sitting room. When Megan joined the rest of them at the kitchen table, Kate told the boys what she had seen.

Anders was buttering a huge slice of Breda's good bread. "Did Megan see them—I mean, hear them?"

Megan turned toward the sound of his voice. "No, I didn't see them."

Anders started to laugh. "See, Kate, you're imagining things again."

But Erik was looking at Megan. "Anders, I don't think you got the point. I think Megan would like to be treated just like the rest of us."

Megan spoke earnestly. "I still have the same feelings as everyone else!" She stopped, as though she had already said too much.

"Last night I promised Megan we'd do everything together," Kate said. She looked from Erik to Anders. "What we do, she does. I promised."

"We'll do *everything* together?" Megan asked, as though she hardly dared believe it.

"Everything," Anders told her. "That's our promise."

When Megan lifted her glass of milk, her hand shook. She tried to smile, but looked closer to tears.

As soon as breakfast was over, Kate slipped away to talk to Willie. She found him feeding the horses.

"You really think you can do everything together?" Willie asked when Kate told him what they planned. "Are you sure that's possible?"

Kate straightened, flipped her braid over her shoulder. "We'll do our best."

"Well—" Willie wasn't convinced. "If that's what you want, then you figure out how to do it."

"I will," Kate said. Not for anything was she going to change her mind. "It'll work. You'll see."

Willie looked as if he didn't believe her, but said no more. Turning his back on Kate, he climbed up to the loft and threw down hay for the horses.

Watching him, Kate felt uneasy. Maybe Willie was right. Again Kate wondered if she could keep her word. She knew she would do everything in her power to try.

* * * * *

Kate and Megan, Anders, Erik, and Willie took the streetcar to the far end of Red Jacket Village. When they reached the Copper Range Depot, the platform was filled with families. One excited person after another called to friends they hadn't seen for some time.

Like Anders and Erik, most of the grown-ups carried large lunch baskets. Many of the people had Willie's dark-haired good looks. Kate wondered if they, too, had come from Cornwall, the peninsula in southwestern England.

"The railroad started service in January," Megan explained. "That's why there's a reunion this year. Before that, it was too hard for people to get back to Central."

Soon the train chugged into the station. Several railroad cars had been added for people coming from all over the Keweenaw Peninsula.

When they climbed aboard, Anders led Kate, Megan, and Erik toward two seats that faced each other. Already Willie had disappeared.

As the train left the depot, Kate peered out the window, trying to see everything she could. When Calumet Township fell behind them, the oak and maple and pine of Michigan's northwoods grew close to the track.

In their railroad car every seat was filled. Before long, one of the men began to sing. All around Kate, others joined in the words of "All Hail the Power of Jesus' Name." The tune was different from the one Kate normally heard.

"It's 'Diadem,' their favorite hymn," Megan explained when Kate asked. "They call it 'Diadem' because that's the name of the tune. Daddy says that's the way Cornishmen sing when they ride down into a mine."

Each time the singers reached the chorus, their deep male voices rumbled on the runs. "Crown Him! Crown Him! And crown Him Lord of all!"

For some time the men continued, with most of the songs being hymns. To Kate it was one of the most special things she had ever heard. She always loved music, but here was something more—the deeply held beliefs of men who lived each day with the dangers of the mines.

As they traveled up the Keweenaw Peninsula, the train often stopped at mining villages to take on passengers. During one of the stops, Kate leaned back against the seat. Directly behind, two men were talking.

"Do you ever hear anything more about that treasure?" one asked.

The other man laughed. "That old story! Wouldn't it be strange, after all these years . . . " His voice faded away as though wishing the story might indeed be true.

"Lots of things stranger than that," the first man answered. "Why, look what happened at Minesota. Can you imagine a mine losing two kegs of silver nuggets? And finding them a couple years after someone misplaced them?"

"But how could old man Mitchell—"

A long whistle drowned out his words. As the train chugged away from the station, Kate strained to hear. By the time she could understand what they were saying, the men were talking about something else.

Twisting around, Kate stole a quick look. She was sure she hadn't seen either of them before.

Treasure, Kate thought. *A lost treasure. And Mr. Mitchell again.*

As though she had heard Willie only moments before, Kate remembered his words on the drive from the depot.

"I'm gonna find me that treasure," he had said.

He had been upset, as though trying to get even with Megan. But did he, too, know a story about a long-ago treasure?

Once again Kate wondered about the people she'd heard on the train from Wisconsin. *What's the secret they know and I don't? Somehow I'm going to find out!*

Central Mine

When they left the train at Central Mine, Willie was nowhere in sight. For a brief moment Kate wondered where he was. Then she felt relieved that he was gone.

It wasn't hard to follow the great crowd of people swarming up the hill. Every now and then someone stopped. With excited voices men and women and children greeted friends and former neighbors.

Megan walked close to the side of the road with her left foot using the grass as a guide. Partway up the steep slope, she turned at a cross street.

"Now, help me count," she asked Kate and the boys. "Tell me every time we come to a house."

When Megan finally stopped, her face glowed with excitement. "This is the house where we lived till I was three years old! Daddy told me how to find it. Willie and his pa lived right next door."

The grass around the house was long, and the gardens overgrown. Sunlight flashed in the bare windows of a home long empty.

"When the mine closed, people moved wherever they could find work," Megan said. "I've always wanted to come back to the place where I was born."

When the boys set down the picnic baskets, Megan took the largest one and put it on the open porch. "After church we can eat at my house." She giggled, as though the idea seemed funny, even to her.

As Anders and Erik walked on, Kate decided that the biggest basket was in a good place. Sheltered by the roof of the porch, it was out of the sun. The cover protected Breda's good lunch from any hungry dog that might come along. But the second basket—the one with Megan's precious cake—had only a cloth across the top.

Not for anything would Kate leave the cake for whatever ants might find the rich pastry. She tried the front door but found it locked. Then she discovered a window that opened. Reaching in, Kate set the cake on the floor, then closed the window again.

On the nearby street, groups of people were moving more quickly, all walking in one direction. Arm in arm, Kate and Megan started after them.

Looking ahead, Kate saw a tall square tower. The white frame building that Megan called Central Methodist Church stood on the side of the hill. Near the front door, a man greeted visitors.

Inside, Kate saw bouquets of black-eyed susans and lacey white wildflowers on a small table near the front. As she led Megan toward the last empty pew, people waited quietly for the service to begin. Yet even here in the church Kate sensed the excitement of people returning for a homecoming.

Soon a woman started playing the reed organ, and the aisle filled with people. When an older couple could not find a place, Kate turned to Megan. "I think we better give them our seat. There's not enough room."

Standing up, Kate led Megan outside. Already, young people filled the grassy hillside across the road from the church. Kate and Megan found Anders and Erik and sat down next to them.

Soon the singing began, pouring out through the open doors and windows. Before long Kate recognized the tune of "Diadem." She wished she were inside the church, hearing the hymn echo off the walls. But then, with one movement, the young people on the hillside stood up and joined the singing.

"Crown Him! Crown Him!" The words filled the hills and valleys with praise. "And crown Him Lord of all!"

As the hymn ended, Kate saw her cousin's face. Silent tears ran down Megan's cheeks.

"It's the music," she whispered when Kate asked if something was wrong. "It's people singing that God is the Lord of *everything!*"

Megan sniffled, blew her nose. "I can't tell you what that means *here*." Lightly she touched her heart.

From inside the church, a strong male voice read aloud from the Bible. Kate knew the verse from the thirty-second chapter of Jeremiah: " 'Behold, I am the Lord, the God of all flesh: is there any thing too hard for me?' "

Megan's lips moved silently as she repeated the words to herself. "*Nothing* is too hard!" she whispered, as though forgetting the people around her. Megan's face shone, as if inside a light had been lit.

After the service, men carried the organ out to the steps, and the soloist sang for those sitting on the grass. Megan seemed to drink in every note. Watching her cousin, Kate hardly dared breathe.

When the last note died away, she and Megan walked back to the house where the O'Connell family had lived.

"I was born in the back bedroom," Megan said. "Let's see how it looks."

Arm in arm, Kate and Megan walked around the outside of the house. In the backyard Megan stopped. "Can I borrow your eyes, Kate?" she asked. "What do you see?"

"A tall house," Kate answered as she noticed a cracked pane of glass. "The paint is faded, but still good."

She wondered how she could make the house special for Megan. "We're standing on a hill," Kate went on.

Megan nodded. "I can feel the slant with my feet."

"There's a tree full of green apples. There are wild daisies blowing in the wind."

Megan lifted her head as though to feel the breeze against her face.

It's beauty she needs, Kate thought, feeling surprised. She tried to notice everything that was beautiful.

"You can see down the hill," Kate went on. "Off in the distance the trees look blue like mountains. The sky is blue too—a brighter blue—with a few white clouds."

Megan sighed. "That's how I thought it would be." Suddenly she turned. "Is the lunch all right?"

"I saw it when we came," Kate answered.

But Megan looked uneasy, as though not satisfied with Kate's answer. As they started around to the front, Erik met them. When Kate stopped to talk, Megan kept on, her fingers feeling the side of the house. In a few minutes Kate heard her call.

Near the front porch Megan stood with outstretched hands, feeling the air, then the floorboards. It took only one glance for Kate to see what was missing.

Quickly she climbed the steps and peered through the window. The basket with the heavy cake was still hidden inside the house. But the larger basket was definitely gone.

"Where is it?" Megan sounded bewildered. "I know I set the basket here."

"You're sure?" Erik asked.

"Yes, I'm sure. I have a very good memory for where I put things. I have to, or I'd never find them again."

"Maybe Anders—" Kate started.

"Maybe Anders what?" he asked as he caught up to them.

"Did you take one of the lunch baskets?" Megan asked.

"Not me!" Anders exclaimed. "I'm planning to eat everything we brought. Is one of them gone?"

"I'm afraid so!" Kate answered. A surge of anger flooded her being. "Willie! It has to be him!"

"Aw, c'mon, Kate, just because you don't like—" Erik said.

"No! That's not it! I mean, it's true that I don't like him, but it's more than that."

"I know what Kate means." Megan's voice held a sadness. "Willie is the only other person who might guess where we put the basket."

"That so?" Anders asked. "Well, we'll take care of this little problem in one minute. Where do you think I'd find him?"

"Right next door," Megan said. "Try the other side of his house."

Anders stalked away, across the overgrown lawn. Kate and the others followed him. They found Willie sitting by himself under the shade of a tree. His dinner pail stood open on the ground before him.

As he reached in to take out the food, Anders stopped in front of him. "Willie!" he said.

As the boy looked up, Anders reached down and snatched the pail. Willie jumped to his feet. "Hey! That's mine!"

"Not anymore," Anders answered calmly. "You took our lunch. We get yours."

"Who said I took your lunch?"

"I said!" Kate stood before him, so angry she could spit. "I said it, and it's true!"

"You can't prove it! You didn't see me!"

"No! But Megan did!" Kate clapped her hand over her mouth. Now she'd done it—making matters even worse between the two of them!

"A blind girl?" Willie scoffed. "She can't see!"

"Oh, yes I can!" Megan's voice was filled with anger. "I heard you, William Henry Pascoe. I heard your step on the porch."

"Ha!"

"You tried not to make a sound, but I knew you were there!"

"You *knew*?" Willie's anger faded from his face, replaced by another look Kate didn't understand.

Then she noticed something—a spot of strawberry jam on Willie's sleeve. "You ate at least one of our sandwiches," Kate said. "I made the strawberry ones myself!"

Willie flushed, but Megan wasn't finished with him. "You're the most obnoxious boy I know!" she cried.

Willie's eyes sparked with anger. He clenched his fists, moved forward. But Anders stepped between them.

"Don't worry!" Willie said. "I'm not going to hit her! Stupid girl!" He stalked off, circled the neighboring house and disappeared.

"He thinks I'm helpless!" Megan stormed. "And I'm not!"

Anders carried Willie's dinner pail to Megan's house. "What a lousy thing to do—taking our lunch!" Anders muttered as they sat down on the back steps. "What's wrong with him anyway?"

"Willie doesn't like himself very much." Already Megan seemed less angry. "Ever since my accident he's been different."

When Anders took off the cover, Kate saw that Willie's pail had two inner sections. From the upper section Anders took out a small cotton sack with a drawstring. Inside was something that looked like a pie folded in half.

"What is it?" Kate asked.

"A pasty, no doubt!" Megan answered, pronouncing the word PASS-tee. "After all, Willie's Cornish!"

Underneath the first pasty was a second one. Anders divided both of them in half.

"You can hold it in your hands," Megan explained when she received her portion. "It's meat and potatoes and onion sealed in a pie crust. And rutabagas too, if a Cousin Jenny makes it."

"A Cousin Jenny?" Kate asked.

"A Cornish woman," Megan explained.

Kate bit into her piece. "This isn't all bad!"

"There must be seedy buns, right?" Megan asked.

Anders looked inside the pail. "Buns with caraway seeds on the top? You betcha! And a yellow cake."

"Saffron cake?" Megan giggled. "We did all right on this one!"

Erik was inspecting the two inner sections of Willie's pail.

"The top part holds the food," Megan explained when Kate asked her about it. "A Cousin Jenny puts tea in the bottom half. The tea helps to keep the pasty warm."

When they finished eating, Megan stood up. "Let's go see the school. People say it's the most beautiful on the Keweenaw Peninsula."

Leaving Anders and Erik behind, the two girls followed the road up the steep hill. The road led them through the woods, then turned left to come out behind the school. Again Megan wanted Kate to talk about the things she saw.

"It's a large three-story building," Kate said as she described the school. She told Megan about the tall pillars that supported the roof over the front entrance.

The front yard of the school extended onto a rock formation. Kate and Megan walked out to where the bluff dropped sharply away. Scattered across the hillside below were homes and other buildings, many of them large and built of rock. For the first time Kate understood how twelve hundred people had once lived at Central.

"Can you see the mine?" Megan asked.

"There are some big buildings," Kate answered. "Would that be it?"

She described what she saw—the distant hills, a tall smokestack, the now empty houses.

"Thanks for lending me your eyes," Megan said finally, and Kate felt warmed by her words. Already she loved her cousin.

Soon they left the school and started back. As they came out of the woods, Kate looked down the hill. Near a butcher shop, someone ducked behind a house.

Who is it? Kate thought, instantly alert. Was someone following her and Megan?

The person had run like a mouse heading for cover. *Why does he have to hide?*

Willie's Story

Kate stared at the house, then the nearby bushes. In the hot July afternoon, the breeze had vanished. Not even a branch moved.

Kate touched Megan's arm. "I see something—someone," Kate warned. "Maybe it's Willie, trying to trick us again."

"Waiting to pounce on us?" Megan asked.

"I don't know." Kate felt silly. She had only a glimpse of the man's shirt. "Maybe it's not anything."

"If it's Willie, I won't worry about it," Megan said.

"I'm not sure it's him." Kate wished they could go back a different way, but there was no other road down the hill.

The person seemed taller than Willie, more the size of a man. The idea of walking past him frightened Kate.

She waited, trying to push aside her uneasiness. Finally she knew they had no choice but to leave.

"If I tell you to run, go as fast as you can!" she told Megan. "Keep hold of my hand. I'll try to run between the holes in the road."

All the way down, Kate looked from left to right, watching between the houses, peering into the bushes. Whoever the stranger was, she didn't want to meet him while she and Megan were alone.

Kate was still looking around when she saw a boy farther down the hill. "There's Willie!" she exclaimed.

Kate felt relieved to see him. At the same time, she couldn't help but wonder if Willie was the person who had ducked behind the house.

"Why don't you ask him to show you the mine?" Megan said. "He knows all about it."

"I can't figure you out," Kate said. "One minute you hate Willie, the next minute you sound—" Kate broke off.

"Like I wish we were friends again?" Megan asked. "Yes, I do."

"But you always act as if you hate him!"

Megan shook her head. "He's the one who dislikes me. Willie hates it when he has to lead me around. He hates the very air I breathe!"

Kate felt bewildered. "I don't think so." She remembered the strange look she had seen on Willie's face more than once.

Megan tried to smile, but a hurt look stayed around her eyes. "You see—" Megan's voice was soft now. "It's me that has a liking for him."

Kate stopped dead still. "Then why do you treat him the way you do? If you like him, why aren't you nicer to him?"

"Like you're nice to Erik?" Megan asked quietly.

Kate stared at her, unable to think of a thing to say.

Megan giggled. "How did I know? That's what you're wondering, isn't it? Your voice gets softer when you talk to him."

Kate's cheeks felt warm with embarrassment. Yes, she did feel different about Erik, different from the way she felt about anyone else. Was it so easy for everyone to see?

When they came to the street that led to the Methodist church, Kate and Megan walked in the opposite direction. Soon Kate saw Willie again.

His shirt was the same blue as the one worn by the person who frightened her. Again Kate wondered if Willie had ducked behind the house. The person had moved so quickly, Kate couldn't be sure.

"Will you show us the mine?" Kate asked when Willie reached them. "Megan says you could explain things really well."

"She did, did she?" Willie stole a quick glance at Megan. "Well, she's right. Pa's a miner, and my Uncle Tom is boss for a day shift."

Willie wasn't boasting, Kate knew, just being honest. But Megan surprised her again.

"How did you like our lunch?" she asked.

"That's for me to know and you to find out," Willie answered. "The basket is on the back step of your house. Are you sure it wasn't there the whole time?"

"It's right where *you* put it," Megan answered. "Too bad you won't be able to eat heavy cake with us."

"Heavy cake?" Willie blurted out. "There wasn't any—" He stopped, knowing he had given himself away.

Megan giggled. "We liked your pasties," she said sweetly. "If you give Kate a good tour of the mine, I'll let you have a piece of cake."

As though wondering if he should make the trade, Willie hesitated.

"If you don't want to eat it . . . " Megan's voice trailed off, as though it was no concern of hers.

Willie shrugged. Then his appetite seemed to get the best of him. Without another word he led them toward a tall building he called the shaft house. "That's where men entered the mine. It's also where the rock came up."

"Rock?" Kate was still watching Willie's every movement, trying to decide if he was the person she'd seen.

"Rock with copper in it. Pa says that Upper Michigan is the only place in the world where there's pure copper. No other minerals in it," he added proudly. "Indians used it just the way it comes out of the ground."

Willie explained how the early miners at Central brought the rock up in kibbles—large barrel-shaped buckets. The longer Willie talked, the more enthusiastic he became. For the first time Kate could understand why he and Megan had been friends. Willie brought the deserted buildings to life.

Listening to him, Kate wished she could go down into a mine, but the shaft house was closed off from any curious eyes. The great stone engine house stood like the homes where people had once lived—a ghost town.

As they started back, they met Anders and Erik.

"Time for cake," Willie announced.

Anders rolled his eyes toward Kate. "Who says there's cake?" he asked Willie. "We ate yours."

"I made Megan a trade. I showed her and Kate the mine."

As Willie had said, the picnic basket was on the back step of Megan's old house. Anders lifted the cover and found some sandwiches inside.

"Glad you left us some," he told Willie. It took no time at all for Anders and Erik to divide the rest of the food between themselves.

As they sat down on the steps, a dog roamed into the yard and headed straight toward Anders. When he held the sandwich safely away, the dog sat down and waited.

Finally Anders stood up. Walking away from the house, he threw bits of food. The dog raced after them.

Kate went around to the front and reached through the window for the heavy cake. The rich pastry looked good, and by now Kate was hungry again. Returning to the others, she set the pan on the wide back step.

Using the fingers of her left hand to measure, Megan held the knife close to her left thumb, then cut large pieces. "First one goes to Willie," she said, and Kate passed it to him.

Willie took an enormous bite. Suddenly he choked, then coughed again. Standing up, he jumped off the step and spit out the cake.

"Willie Pascoe!" Megan exclaimed. "What are you doing with my good cake?"

"You are absolutely awful!" Kate told him. "How can you be so terrible when Megan worked so hard—"

Willie choked again. Kate turned her back, ignoring him. She handed a piece to Erik.

He took one small bite, and swallowed it quickly. "You're a good cook, Megan," he said solemnly. Leaning back against the house, he held the cake carefully in his hand.

As soon as Anders returned to the steps, Kate gave him a piece. Again the dog moved close to Anders and waited.

Like Willie, Anders took a big bite. In the next instant, his cheeks and eyes bugged out as if the cake were stuck in his throat. With a great effort he swallowed.

A moment later, Anders stretched back his arm and threw the rest of his piece across the yard. As the cake landed in the long grass, the dog bounded off. But when he reached the cake, he sniffed, then walked away.

Anders made the worst face Kate had ever seen. Finger to her lips as though shushing him, she warned him to be quiet. Just because it was something her brother had never eaten, he didn't have to be rude.

"It's really good cake, Megan," Anders said just as solemnly as Erik.

"Thanks, Anders," Megan answered. "I'm glad you like it."

"Oh, I do," Anders said. "It must have taken you a long time to learn how to make something that good."

As soon as Megan sat down, Kate took her own piece. *Stupid boys!* she thought. She hoped Megan wouldn't guess how they really felt.

Kate bit into her cake. Suddenly she clutched her throat, trying to swallow.

Just then Megan took her first bite. "This is awful!" she exclaimed. "How could you eat it?"

Kate grabbed a napkin. "It *is* a bit salty, Megan!"

"A bit! I must have used salt instead of sugar! I put almost a cup of salt in that cake!"

Megan jumped up. "I am *so* embarrassed! Willie, I made that cake because it's your favorite!"

"You did?" Willie seemed to soften. Now that he'd gotten rid of his piece, his color had returned to normal.

"How could I do such a stupid thing?" Megan wailed.

"Hey, Megan!" Anders reached out, caught her hand, and pulled her back to the step. "Now we know you're not perfect."

"I'm not perfect, all right!"

"Hey, listen to me," Anders said. "You do so many things well, it's good to know you're just like us."

"Like you?"

"Yah, sure. You betcha."

"You really mean that, Anders?"

"I mean that." Anders sounded as serious as he'd ever been.

Megan giggled. "You threw your cake away, didn't you?"

"Huh?" Anders stared at her. "How did you know?"

"That dog left one minute after you got your piece."

* * * * *

They were still sitting on the steps when Kate asked, "Willie, did you ever hear a story about a lost treasure?"

"Sure," Willie answered. "The man who owned the treasure lived next door to us."

"Really?" Kate asked. "Right next door to you?"

Willie jumped up. "C'mon. I'll show you." He led them around his house to the one beyond. It looked just like Megan's old house except that it was reddish brown instead of dark gray.

"The man lived here before the people that we knew," Willie said as he dropped down on the front porch.

"What do you know about him?" Kate asked. She and the others sat down near Willie.

"When Pa and I left Central, I was only four years old," he said. "There was a boy who lived in this house. He told me the story of the lost treasure.

"A lot of mines—Cliff, Minesota, and Central are some—had pure silver close to the surface. The silver was mixed right into the rock along with the copper. When the miners found silver, they took out those pieces of rock in their dinner pails."

"Isn't that stealing?" Kate asked.

Willie shrugged. "Pa says that even the mining companies sometimes wondered. Papers for Michigan mines say they're formed for mining copper. So if miners found silver, they played finders keepers. Part of the game was not showing the boss the prize. If the boss saw the silver, the miner gave it up. But if he didn't—" Willie grinned.

He leaned back against a post, made himself comfortable. "Once upon a time," he began, "there was a miner named Ellis. Ellis was a poor man. When he found silver, only his partner knew. They carried it out in their dinner pails. At night Ellis and his partner covered the windows. By the light of a candle they broke the silver out of the rock."

Willie knocked on the wooden porch. *Tap-tap! Tap-tap!*

"Night after night, Ellis and his partner worked." *Tap-tap! Tap-tap!* "All the neighbors heard their hammers. All the neighbors knew. For didn't they also break silver out of rock when they found it? At last Ellis and his partner had a keg filled with silver nuggets."

"A *whole* keg?" Anders broke in.

"That's how the story goes." Willie clearly did not like being interrupted. "They divided the silver into two kegs and hid it away. Then one day Ellis's partner died in a mine accident. Ellis barely escaped himself. Soon after, Ellis told his boss he had to leave for a time. His brother was real sick and wanted to see him. Ellis caught a ride on a supply wagon to Red Jacket. He took only the knapsack on his back."

"No treasure?" Kate asked softly.

"No treasure."

"Ellis went to a man by the name of Mitchell—"

This time even Anders sat up straight.

9

More Trouble

"The Mitchell we know?" Kate asked.

"His father Samuel," Willie said. "Sam Mitchell had helped Ellis when he needed money. Ellis hadn't been able to pay it back. Now Ellis told Mitchell that his brother was sick. He borrowed still more money—the train fare—from Mr. Mitchell.

"When he left, Ellis gave Mitchell a map. 'If I don't come back, use it,' he said. 'You'll get the money I owe and then some.'

"Mr. Mitchell put the map away. As the story goes, he even forgot about it. In 1895, after building the mansion in Laurium, he found the map. One day he decided to do something about it. He told the man who worked for him to hitch up the horses. They were going to take a look around. 'We'll see what kind of treasure we find!' he said.

"While the driver hitched up the horses, Mr. Mitchell went back into the mansion for the map. The driver waited and waited. Finally he went to look for Mr. Mitchell. The old man had collapsed and died."

"And the driver got the treasure?" Erik asked.

"Nope! He was the one who first told the story. People from Central added what they knew. As far as anyone knows, no one ever found the map. So," Willie said, "that's the story of the man who never came back—not even for a treasure!"

In spite of the sunshine, Kate shivered. Then she glanced at Megan. Megan looked as though she were trying not to laugh.

Willie glanced her way. "You don't believe me?" he asked stiffly. "Where the man went and where he is now, nobody knows."

From low in his throat Anders offered an ominous chuckle.

Willie turned on him. "You don't believe me either!"

Anders shook his head, grinned. "Nope! But it's a good story."

"And you, Erik?"

"Wellll—" Erik winked at Kate.

But Kate was curious. "Willie, this morning I heard a man on the train. He was talking about that story."

Willie looked relieved, as if glad that at least one person believed him.

Kate leaned forward. "If you believe the story is true, have you looked in the house?"

Willie shook his head. "The family that lived here searched every inch. They even took up the floorboards."

"But why hasn't someone found the silver in all these years? Where could Ellis have hidden it?"

Willie shrugged. "He might have dug a hole in the backyard."

"Wouldn't someone see the mark in the grass?" Kate asked. "The place where he dug?"

"Maybe," Willie answered. "Maybe not."

"What do you mean?" Kate could tell Willie had been thinking about this.

"Say he planted a flower garden on top of the kegs of silver. Harder to find, huh? Or a vegetable garden? All he'd have to do is bury the two kegs deeper than what people dig for a garden."

Kate jumped up. She and the others walked around to the backyard. Tall purple flowers bloomed above the long grass. One red rose tried to find its way through the weeds.

Near where Kate stood, asparagus had gone to seed. Raspberry bushes offered painful thorns.

"Ellis could make it even harder to find," Erik said. He looked toward the hills. "Maybe he hid the treasure in the woods. There are an awful lot of trees around here, away from town."

"If only we knew how much time Ellis had to hide the silver," Megan said.

Willie turned toward her, alert and interested.

"If we knew that," Megan went on, "it would help us know where to look."

"You're right!" Willie stared at Megan as though seeing her for the first time. "Why didn't I think of that before?"

Megan smiled. "Because you didn't ask *me*."

She was teasing, Kate knew, yet something had changed between them. Kate wondered about it. If Megan and Willie had known each other all these years, why weren't they friendly more often?

"Megan, where would *you* look for the silver?" Willie was serious now, as though he really thought she could tell him.

"I'd try the yard first," Megan said. "If ground was dug up, it might sink just slightly."

Willie grinned. "Now *that's* a good idea!"

"I could feel a dip in the ground better than anyone," Megan said. "If someone walks with me to be sure I cover every part of the yard—"

"I'll do it!" Willie said. "Let's start right now."

Arm in arm, Megan and Willie walked across the yard, starting at one corner and working their way toward the other. They had almost finished searching when a train whistle sounded from below the hill.

Across the street a woman called her children, then gathered up her picnic basket. People started to stroll past, heading for the depot. More than once, Kate saw a family turn back for a last look at the home where they had once lived.

In spite of what he'd said about finding his own friends, Willie rode with them on the train back to Red Jacket. During the entire trip he was strangely quiet. Kate wondered if he was thinking about the treasure.

"Maybe the map is still hidden away in the mansion," Kate told Megan when they returned home. "Is there some way we could get in there and search?"

* * * * *

In the middle of the night Kate once again woke up. She rubbed her eyes, then looked out the window. No voices spoke from the darkness.

Even so, Kate couldn't go back to sleep. Something still bothered her. Why did Megan and Willie act the way they did? One moment they seemed to hate each other. The next moment they acted like old friends.

Early the next morning Kate slipped out to the stable. She found Willie in one of the stalls, brushing down a gray mare. Willie looked up, but kept on working.

"I just don't understand you," Kate said after watching for a while. "Sometimes you're fun to know. Other times—" Kate stopped, not wanting to make things worse.

But Willie said it for her. "Other times I'm a stinker?"

"Why do you and Megan fight so much?" Kate asked. "Have you always been that way?"

A strange look passed through Willie's eyes. "We used to be good friends," he said.

"What happened?" Kate asked.

"Megan got hurt," Willie answered, as though that explained everything.

"Blind, you mean? But she can still do all kinds of things. Look at how she found her way around yesterday."

Willie nodded. "In spite of me."

Once again the strange look passed across Willie's face. This time Kate recognized it for what it was. Pain unlike anything she had ever seen.

"I can't stand it!" Willie exclaimed. "Every time I look at Megan, I remember. I'm the one who made her blind!"

His lips quivered. As though ashamed to be caught crying, he whirled around. His arms over his head, he buried his face in the mane of the horse.

Kate's insides twisted into a knot. Afraid to move or speak, she waited. She had never seen a boy sob as Willie did. His weeping seemed to fill the quiet stable.

When at last he turned from the horse, Willie's face and eyes were red, his hair twisted every which way. "It's my fault that Megan is blind!"

Kate's gaze met his. "I don't believe that!"

"I was ten years old," Willie said. "I'd been driving horses for over a year. I should have kept them steady."

"No!" Kate answered.

"It's my fault the horses moved."

"No, no, no!" Kate exclaimed. "Megan says she stood up before the wagon stopped."

Willie stared at Kate. "Megan said *that*?"

"She said the accident was *her* fault. Not the horses'. Not yours. *Her* fault."

"You're sure?" Willie seemed unable to take in Kate's words.

"What can I say to make you believe me?" she asked.

"Tell me again!" Willie asked. "Tell me again what Megan said!"

When Kate finished, Willie looked as if a hundred-pound weight had fallen from his shoulders. "All this time I could never stop feeling awful." His words tumbled out. "I couldn't stand to look at Megan. I hated myself for what I had done."

Reaching out, Kate put her hand on his arm. "Willie, even if it had been your fault, accidents happen. Something like that could happen to anyone. You didn't mean to do it. You didn't try to do it."

Again Willie's dark eyes filled with tears. He struggled against them, but this time didn't turn away.

"Willie," Kate said softly. "Have you ever talked to Megan about the whole thing?"

Willie shook his head.

"You can't just run away," Kate said.

"I know. It's always there between us."

"Even when something is an accident, you need to be responsible," Kate answered. "Even though it wasn't your fault, you need to say you're sorry."

Willie's gaze clung to Kate's. For the first time his eyes held a ray of hope.

"Why don't you *really* talk to Megan?" Kate said.

* * * * *

"Megan, me girl," Breda said at the breakfast table. "There's a big dinner party at the mansion tonight. I don't like to ask when Kate's here, but we need some extra help."

Megan groaned. "Oh, Ma."

"If you work hard this morning, you can be done by noon."

"What do you do?" Kate asked. Under the table Kate kicked her cousin's foot.

"Dust and clean—whatever needs doing." As if suddenly remembering Kate's desire to search the mansion, Megan turned to her mother. "Can Kate help me?"

"I'll dust real fast so Megan gets done quicker," Kate said.

But Megan shook her head. "We can't dust fast. You'll see."

Once in the mansion, Kate discovered that cleaning wasn't as easy as it sounded. For one thing Tisha, the housekeeper, expected everything to be perfect.

In a gray uniform with a white apron, Tisha looked even more stern than she had when coming from the depot. She started by asking Megan to sweep the kitchen.

Megan found the broom and set a kitchen chair in the middle of the floor. Moving around the room, she swept toward the chair, then used the dustpan.

When Megan finished, the floor looked spotless, but Tisha only said, "That will do. Now you can dust both upstairs and down."

Tisha looked down her straight nose at Kate. "Why are you here? Megan needs to work."

"I'll help," Kate said.

"Make sure you don't break anything," Tisha answered.

Her cold blue eyes made Kate nervous. "I'll be careful," Kate promised.

When she and Megan entered the parlor, Kate understood why they couldn't dust fast. Fragile lamps stood on the highly polished tables. Crystal vases made Kate feel as if she had entered a room filled with glass.

Megan showed her what to do. With both hands she lifted a lamp and set it carefully out of the way. Using a soft cloth, she dusted across the width of the table, going all one way. Then she dusted the table a second time, this time across the length. When she finished, the table shone.

Megan replaced the lamp and they went on to the library. Kate found it heavy with the scent of cigar smoke.

"This is where the men talk after a big dinner," Megan explained as she opened the windows. "The women wait in the parlor while the men have their smoke."

Kate had seen this many books in only one place—the Minneapolis Public Library. She decided it would be an excellent place to hide a treasure map.

"Mrs. Mitchell lets us borrow any book we want," Megan said.

"I'll come back," Kate said, hoping she'd have a chance to look through every book. "I'll find a book I can read to you."

Minutes later, Breda asked Megan to go to the grocery store for food needed for the dinner. When Megan left, Kate kept dusting. Before long, she finished the library and went on to the music room.

There she found a large square grand piano. Kate dusted between the black keys, then up and down the keyboard. The piano had the most beautiful sound she had ever heard.

At home Kate had a reed organ. She had played a piano only a few times, and never one like this. Unable to resist the temptation, she sat down and started playing songs she knew from memory. At first she played softly, hoping no one would hear. Before long, Kate forgot where she was.

Suddenly she realized that someone was standing behind her. Twirling around on the piano stool, she looked up at Mrs. Mitchell.

"I'm sorry!" Kate's cheeks felt warm with embarrassment. "I forgot I'm supposed to be dusting."

"I'm glad you did," Mrs. Mitchell said. "What a treat to hear you play!"

"It was?"

"You have a beautiful touch. I felt as if I were hearing your heart."

"Thank you," Kate said, because she knew she should. But the words seemed too simple for all she was feeling.

"Come over and use the piano while you're here," Mrs. Mitchell told her.

"Really?" Kate couldn't believe her ears. She went back to her dusting, but could hardly wait to try the piano again.

Kate was in the kitchen helping Breda and Tisha when Megan and Willie burst in. Willie carried a basket of groceries, but his eyes looked scared. One glance at Megan, and Kate understood why.

A large patch of dirt covered her dress as if she had fallen. Her black hair had slipped out of its braid. Streaks of dirt lined her cheeks.

The Mansion's Secrets

One of Megan's arms was bleeding, scraped raw where she had fallen.

"Megan, me darlin'!" Breda threw her arms around her daughter. Standing in the middle of the kitchen floor, Breda rocked Megan back and forth as if she were a small child.

"What happened?" Breda asked finally, just as Mrs. Mitchell entered the kitchen.

With one look at Megan the woman hurried out. By the time she returned with her husband, Megan could tell them what was wrong.

"I gave the grocery man the list, and he filled it," she said. "After I left the store, a man spoke to me. He asked, 'You're visiting Casey O'Connell?' I tried to tell him that he's my daddy, but the man kept talking. When he started to come closer, I ran."

Megan drew a long shuddering breath. "I heard footsteps behind me. I didn't notice where I was going till I landed on the sidewalk. When I fell, the footsteps stopped. I didn't know if that awful man was still around."

Megan felt her arm, being careful not to touch the place where it was scraped. "I tried to tell myself that I could get home. But I kept wondering about that man. Was he still there, watching me?"

"He must have thought you were me!" Kate exclaimed.

"Are you sure you're all right?" Mr. Mitchell asked Megan.

She nodded, but she still looked afraid.

"The man talked about your father by name?" Mr. Mitchell sounded as if he wanted to be sure.

Again Megan nodded.

"After you fell, what happened?"

"Willie came," Megan answered. "I was so glad to see him!"

"You *saw* him?" Mr. Mitchell sounded puzzled.

"I knew it was him by his voice. I knew he was scared too. He helped me up and said the man was nowhere around. He walked me home."

Mr. Mitchell turned toward Willie. "Did you see the man at all?"

"No, sir," Willie answered respectfully. He still looked upset by what had happened to Megan.

"Where was Megan when you found her?"

"A block and a half on the other side of the store. She had gone the opposite way—toward Red Jacket. Toward my house, instead of here."

"I was so scared, I got turned around," Megan explained.

"It was the first time I've ever seen her lost," Willie said. Something had changed in the way he looked at Megan, as though he'd grown up in that terrible moment when he found her so afraid.

"Have you been lost before?" Mr. Mitchell asked Megan.

"I like to do errands," she said quickly, as if afraid she'd no longer be allowed to go. "I count blocks. I know where a dog always barks, where a woman bakes bread. When I come to the right block, I count doorways. It's not hard finding the grocery store."

"Have you told us everything that happened?" Mr. Mitchell asked gently.

Megan started to speak, then stopped, bit her lip.

"We want to make sure this doesn't happen again," Mr. Mitchell said. "Why do you think the man wanted to talk to Kate?"

"He just said, 'I wanna know what you found at Central.'"

A sudden crash broke into Megan's words. "Sorry!" Tisha exclaimed. A vase had slipped from her hands, splintering into pieces all over the floor.

As if there had been no interruption, Mr. Mitchell asked another question. "Could you recognize the man who spoke to you?"

"I'll never forget his voice," Megan answered. "He'd been drinking enough to slur his words. Maybe that's why he talked to me."

For a moment Megan was silent, as though trying hard to remember. "There was something else," she said slowly. "A smell I didn't recognize. But I'll know if I ever smell it again."

"It's that old story!" Mrs. Mitchell spoke for the first time since bringing her husband to the kitchen.

"Supposedly a man named Ellis gave my father a map," Mr. Mitchell told Kate. "Ellis said the treasure would pay back the money he owed and more."

Mr. Mitchell sighed. "At least that's the way I heard the story. Whether it's true or false, I don't know."

"Your father didn't tell you?" Kate asked.

"I was away at school at the time." Mr. Mitchell rubbed his chin. "It could have slipped my father's mind as not being important. After he died, I came back and took over the business. Got married."

He glanced toward Mrs. Mitchell. "My wife went through the house, moved out old furniture, and made the mansion a home. It was five years before I heard the story."

"Maybe Kate can find the map," Megan said quickly. "Erik said she and Anders have solved a lot of mysteries."

"With Erik's help!" Kate exclaimed.

But Mr. Mitchell shook his head. "We've looked everywhere, but there's not a trace!"

When Breda left to take Megan home, Mr. Mitchell asked them to send over Anders and Erik.

"I want to work out a plan," Mr. Mitchell said as soon as the boys arrived. "Tomorrow my wife and I need to leave town on business."

"I'm afraid to go on a trip." Worry lined Mrs. Mitchell's face. "We've found out how awful that story is. Twice, when it made the rounds, someone broke in."

Mrs. Mitchell glanced toward the housekeeper. Tisha was still cleaning up glass as if that were her only concern. But Kate could tell she was listening.

"Usually Tisha takes care of everything," Mrs. Mitchell went on. "She's the best housekeeper I've ever had. But I promised she could visit her mother while we're gone."

"Is that where you were before?" Kate asked Tisha. "When we came in on the train?"

"Certainly!" Tisha's cold blue eyes met Kate's. "My mother has been ill."

Tisha's look made Kate feel uneasy. It was as though the housekeeper thought Kate was snooping into her private affairs. Kate was glad when Tisha left the room.

"On some of the days I'm gone, Casey will also be away, looking after things for me," Mr. Mitchell said. He asked if Kate and the boys would turn on lights and walk through the house now and then.

"You betcha!" Anders did his best to look responsible. "We'll make it look as if there are a lot of people here." Already he was eyeing the room, as though deciding where he'd search first.

Erik stepped forward. "You know, Mr. Mitchell, there's another way we can help you."

"That so?"

"Suppose the map really is hidden here."

"We've even hired a detective to search the house," Mr. Mitchell answered. "We wanted to stop the stories."

"Maybe someone with different eyes, looking in a different way—"

Mr. Mitchell smiled. "Are you asking my permission? If so, you're welcome to search the house while we're gone."

Erik grinned. "Yes, sir."

"Look anywhere you like, from top to bottom!" Mrs. Mitchell added.

"We'll do our best," Erik promised. "I just hope we find something."

"If you don't, you'll still have helped us," Mr. Mitchell said. "If people see you around, they'll think we're home."

Erik grinned at Kate, as though he had just handed her a present. He had! Erik knew how curious Kate was.

She could hardly wait to begin. "We'll start searching as soon as you leave. When you come back, maybe we'll have good news!"

"Maybe you will," Mrs. Mitchell said gently but without much hope.

Mr. Mitchell slipped a watch out of his vest pocket. "Willie, make sure the horses get exercise while I'm gone."

"Yes, *sir*."

"But don't run them too hard."

"I'll take good care of them," Willie promised.

"We'll help him," Anders said solemnly.

A spark of humor flashed through Mr. Mitchell's eyes. "I'm sure you will," he said dryly. "And I'm sure you won't dare him to do something he shouldn't."

Anders flushed, as though knowing he had been warned.

"I won't feel safe until that treasure is found," Mrs. Mitchell said.

"Neither will Megan," Willie answered. "She'll never know if that man is somewhere around, watching her."

Kate didn't like that idea at all. "If we don't find that map, Megan might never be safe again."

* * * * *

When Kate returned to the carriage house Megan had washed her face and changed her clothes. A bandage covered the scrape on her arm.

The look on Megan's face told Kate that her cousin was still scared, but trying not to show it.

"Megan—" Kate heard the uncertainty in her own voice. She didn't want to frighten her cousin still more. Yet Kate knew she'd never forgive herself if she didn't do her best to protect Megan.

"Has anyone ever bothered you before?" Kate asked.

Megan shook her head.

"Then let's make sure it doesn't happen again. I think the man thought you were me."

"Do we really truly look that much alike?" Megan asked.

Kate nodded, then changed to the teasing voice Megan liked. "Really truly. We're almost exactly the same height. We've both got the black hair and deep blue eyes of the dark Irish. The only big difference if someone doesn't know us is the way you used to braid your hair."

But when Kate suggested that her cousin have two braids again, Megan said, "No! It's fun wearing one braid just like you." Though Kate tried, she couldn't change Megan's mind.

In the end it was Willie who succeeded. "I can't be around watching out for you every minute," he warned.

"I don't *want* you watching out every minute." Megan sounded like her old stubborn self.

"Megan, me girl—" Willie's voice changed to a perfect imitation of her father Casey. "It's blarney you're speaking, and yourself knows it. You really don't care if a man who tips the bottle speaks to you now and then?"

For an instant the scared look was back in Megan's face. Then she spoke. "Aw, Willie, you haven't got the sound of the Irish, now really, have you?"

But Willie didn't back down. "Kate's right," he said. "Go back to wearing two braids so I can pull both of them."

Megan's laugh sounded like her old self. The next time she braided her hair she did as Willie said.

* * * * *

The next morning Willie drove the Mitchells and Tisha to the railroad station. Kate, Anders, and Erik followed Megan to the mansion. When she unlocked the door, they slipped inside.

In the large kitchen Kate looked around. "Where do we start?"

"In the other rooms," Erik said. "No one would hide something here. The cook would find it too easily."

Anders agreed. "We're talking about something that's been hidden quite a while. The map has to be in a place no one would think of."

Beyond the kitchen was a sunny room where the Mitchell family ate breakfast. As Anders and Erik started looking through the cabinets along one wall, Kate noticed a small desk.

She searched the inside, then stood back. Instead of being in the middle of a wall, the desk was set off center, close to a dark corner. Was there a reason?

Moving forward, Kate checked the wooden panel on one side of the desk. It was smooth and unbroken, even by decoration. Yet when Kate looked at the side of the desk toward the corner, she saw a drawer almost hidden by shadows.

With growing excitement, she knelt down and opened the drawer. It held no treasure—only two bottles of ink and some quill pens.

Too bad! Kate thought. It had looked so promising!

Standing up, she pushed aside the curtain on a nearby window. The July heat reached even here, in the dimness of the mansion. Kate unlocked the window and pushed it open to catch the breeze.

When they went on to the dining room, there was paneling about two thirds of the way up the wall. As though she had dusted it often, Megan ran her hand over the paneling.

"I'll tap the wood," she said. "If there's anything hollow, I'll find it."

The table was big enough to seat fifteen or eighteen people. Beneath the table, a large rug covered the polished floor. The colors of the rug had faded slightly, as if it had been there for a long time.

"Now that looks like a good place to hide something!" Kate exclaimed. "Right under that rug!"

She set the centerpiece and tall silver candlesticks in the next room. She and Anders and Erik moved the table to one side, then rolled up the rug. Underneath, the floor was smooth, unbroken by a loose plank or small trapdoor.

While they moved the table back, Megan continued tapping her way around the room. As Kate set the candlesticks in place, Megan cried out, "I found something! Listen!"

Megan tapped an area above a cupboard. "It's hollow!"

Her sensitive fingers touched a small panel where it lay between wooden crosspieces. Gently she pushed around the edges. Suddenly something clicked!

The Hiding Place

As if hinged from behind, the panel swung inward. "It's a door!" Kate felt like shouting. "You found a secret hiding place!"

Megan's face shone. She reached in to explore a small space. "It's plenty big for a map!"

Her hand moved back and forth, then up and around. A second, then a third time, Megan felt the space. Looking disappointed, she finally stood back. "I don't think there's anything there. Kate, you look."

The space was about four inches deep, a foot or so long, and another foot high. Kate lit a candle to make sure she wasn't missing something. Every board fit tightly against the next. Nothing could have slid down between the cracks.

"Well, Megan, it sure was a good find," Erik said at last.

"It was, wasn't it?" Megan looked happy again, even though the hiding place was empty.

"If there's one secret place, there might be more," Kate said.

For the rest of the morning they searched the downstairs. In the library they took down every book and opened it. One book had pages glued together and a hollow carved out. It was filled with money, but no map. They returned the book and its money to the shelf.

After lunch they searched upstairs. In the master bedroom they discovered a safe hidden beneath a painting, but that was all.

Finally they had to give up. "Tomorrow we'll try the attic and the other buildings," Kate said as they walked back to the O'Connells' apartment. They all agreed that something could be hidden in the stable or the bottom half of the carriage house.

As the sun dropped low in the west, Kate remembered she had forgotten to close the window she had opened in the mansion. Megan gave her the key, and Kate ran back.

The side door unlocked easily. Kate stepped into the back hall where the servants' stairway led upward. Another set of stairs led down to the basement. Both stairways ended in deep shadows.

Without the others along, the house seemed dark and empty. Kate started through the rooms, then remembered that she had promised to find Megan a book. When Kate reached the library, it was strangely still. Unlike that morning, it no longer smelled heavy with cigar smoke.

Kate headed toward the shelves of fiction. On the way there, she passed a table with a book lying on it. The title caught her attention: *The Vanishing Smugglers*.

Aha! Kate thought. She would go no farther. What could be more exciting than to read about smugglers?

Taking the book with her, Kate hurried back toward the breakfast room and the small desk.

Pushing aside the curtain, Kate reached up to shut the window. It was already closed and locked.

Puzzled, Kate stepped back and looked around. She was sure this was the right window. Nearby, another window was also closed and locked.

Through its glass, Kate saw that the evening was rapidly changing to night. Clutching the book she had taken from the library, Kate bolted out of the room. As though someone were chasing her, she hurried through the kitchen.

By the time she reached the back entry, she felt silly and told herself to slow down. Just the same, she quickly locked the door and raced around the back of the mansion. When she reached the carriage house, Kate took the stairs two at a time.

Erik met her on the landing. "A bear chasing you, Kate?"

Without answering, Kate hurried into the apartment. "I left the window open. I'm sure I did! But it was closed and locked!"

"Aw, Kate!" Anders was on the sitting room floor. "You're imagining things!"

Megan came to Kate's defense. "Imagining things, is it?"

Anders groaned. "It's bad enough having one of you, Kate, let alone *two*!"

Megan laughed. "And I'm happy if you think I'm that much like her. Now, Kate, tell us again what happened."

Dropping down beside Megan, Kate started over. This time she remembered the book she planned to read to her cousin. "It was lying on a table in the library."

"It was?" Megan asked. "Usually everything is put away for a dinner party." She thought about it a moment, then shrugged. "Maybe one of the men took it out."

After supper, Kate read to Megan about the smugglers of Cornwall in southwestern England. Soon Erik and Anders joined them at the round oak table in the kitchen.

When Willie stopped in, Kate's gaze met his. *He's here to talk to Megan about the accident! How can I make sure that he does?*

Kate went back to reading aloud: " 'On a dark, moonless night, smugglers roamed the seas around the rocky coasts of Cornwall.' "

Kate's voice dropped to a hoarse whisper. " 'To avoid paying a heavy tax, they sailed their ship into a quiet cove and unloaded. Men on shore carried kegs of spirits and other smuggled goods to a hiding place. When they felt it was safe, they moved the smuggled goods along.' "

"Spirits?" Megan asked. "What are they?"

"Alcoholic beverages," Anders told her.

Kate continued reading: " 'Government boats patrolled the rocky coast, hoping to arrest the smugglers. If warned by a signal fire along the shore, the smugglers slipped out to sea. With their fast ships, they did their best to outrun the patrols.

" 'When necessary, smugglers lowered kegs over the side of their boat into the water. These kegs were tied together with ropes. Stones weighed them down, holding the kegs close to the bottom of the sea. If the loot was not found by government men, the smugglers returned later to rescue it.' "

As Kate finished reading, Anders laughed. "Mighty good way to hide something."

Willie's grin flashed. "Great story!"

Erik liked the way one smuggler had boldly hauled his cargo through the main street of a town. "It looked like a normal wagon load instead of someone hiding something!"

Willie was watching Megan as though he wanted to talk with her. He seemed like a different person from the boy who had met them at the train depot.

Kate jumped up. "Let's go for a walk," she said to Erik.

As Kate hoped, Willie and Megan soon dropped behind. She also hoped that somehow Anders would get lost. Instead, he kept up with her and Erik every step of the way.

When at last they returned to the carriage house, Erik pulled Kate aside. "Wait a minute," he said.

He and Kate sat down, partway up the flight of steps, and away from the open door at the top. After the heat of the day, Kate welcomed the cooler evening. A gentle breeze lifted the hair around her face.

The moonlight fell on Erik's face, and Kate saw that he was watching her.

"Kate, I still want to know. What happened when you went to River Falls?"

In the stillness Kate's heart quivered. At the same time she felt scared to tell Erik how much his friendship meant to her.

"It was good coming home," she said, as if she didn't understand his question. "I liked being back at Windy Hill Farm."

Erik looked disappointed. "Aren't you going to tell me what happened with Michael Reilly?"

"M.R.?" That was what Kate had learned to call him. "Sometime," she said, trying to sound calm. Yet her heart was thumping.

"*Sometime?*" Erik asked. "How about right now?"

As though it had happened only moments before, Kate remembered all that M.R. had said. How could she put that into words?

But Erik was waiting, his gaze searching her face. For some time now, he had been a special friend. He had the right to know.

"When I was in River Falls, I had to make a choice," Kate said, her voice low. "I had to ask myself what I believed."

Her lips trembled, and Kate told herself she would not cry. Yet her words sounded shaky, even to her. "I had to decide what was important to me."

Erik leaned forward, his eyes intent on her face. "And?" he asked when she could not go on.

Kate drew a deep breath. "I knew that what I decided would make a difference the rest of my life."

She paused, waited for her heart to stop thumping. When it didn't, she tried to go on. "What would you say if I told you—"

Again Kate stopped, tried to think how to tell him what mattered most now. Erik waited. Finally Kate knew how to say it. "When I grow up, I'd like to marry a boy who believes the way I do."

In the moonlight Erik's smile was soft. "Thanks, Kate," he said quietly. "That's what I wanted to know."

* * * * *

The next morning Kate and Anders, Erik and Megan started their search at the stable. Willie was already working and helped them look through the main floor.

When they found nothing out of the ordinary, Kate climbed the ladder to the loft. Seeing all the hay, she groaned. Though the loft wasn't as big as the one at Windy Hill Farm, it would be just as hopeless to find something.

Willie came up the ladder behind Kate. "You don't have to look through all that," he said.

"You're sure?" she asked. As overwhelming as the task seemed, she didn't want to miss anything.

"It's first-crop hay," Willie answered. "I helped 'em put it up soon after I started working here. Before that, the loft was almost empty. I would have seen anything that was here."

He started back down the ladder, then turned to look at her. "Thanks, Kate. Thanks for yesterday."

"Did you get it straightened out with Megan?"

Willie nodded. "Maybe now we'll be friends again."

He led Kate and the others over to search the lower half of the carriage house. They came first to the three-seated buggy in which they had come from the train station. Next to that was the most elegant carriage Kate had ever seen. Large oil-burning lamps were mounted on both sides of the front seat.

Beyond that, Anders and Erik were already inspecting a Chalmers, a magnificent automobile.

"Do you ever get to drive it?" Anders asked.

Willie started to say yes, then glanced at Megan. "Nope!" he answered, as though trying to put his bragging behind. "Only Megan's dad drives this."

The sides and fenders were black and shiny, as though someone had just polished every inch with a dust cloth. The glass of the great lights sparkled in the sunlight.

As Anders climbed into the driver's seat, Kate noticed something else. In a dark corner was a bicycle built for two—two handlebars, two seats, two sets of peddles. But only the first rider could steer.

Judging by the dust on the bicycle, it hadn't been used for some time. The chain was off, and both tires were flat, but the bicycle looked as if it wouldn't be hard to fix.

"See what I found!" Kate whispered when Erik came over to ask what she was doing. "Can you make it work again?"

Erik's eyes gleamed. Kate didn't even need to tell him what she was thinking.

"I'll get tools from Willie," he said. "Anders and I can fix it in no time."

Quietly Kate moved away from the bicycle. When she reached Megan, Kate caught her cousin's hand. "Let's look around outside," she said.

The garden between the carriage house and mansion was shaped like a large pie. As if they were slices in the pie, paths ran from the edges of the garden, meeting in the middle.

"Isn't it beautiful?" Megan asked as they walked along a path. She was happier today, and Kate felt sure it was because of her talk with Willie.

"Smell the roses!" Megan said soon. "Are they deep red?" She leaned down, found a stem, and sniffed.

"There are pink roses, too," Kate said, remembering Megan's craving for beauty. "And right next to them, some tall blue flowers."

When they reached the center of the garden, Kate knelt down to look at the birdbath from every angle. She even tipped it slightly to see if anything could be hidden underneath.

From there Kate checked out the two-foot-high wall on the street side of the yard. Every stone was solid, as though none had been moved since the beginning of time. But the stones gave Kate an idea.

"Let's walk around the mansion and see if there's anything loose," she said.

With Megan's hand on her shoulder, Kate looked for any crack between the wood walls and sandstone foundation. She searched first on the side toward the garden and carriage house. Then she and Megan followed the large porch around the front to the other side of the mansion.

There, close to the pillars that supported the roof over the driveway, Kate saw a circle of flowers. Bricks, laid three high, bordered the flowers. As Kate searched, she found one brick just a hair's breadth farther out than the rest.

When she tugged at the brick, it moved easily, then slid out. A folded piece of paper lay underneath.

"I found it!" Kate exclaimed. "I found the map!"

Footsteps in the Dark

Kate picked up the piece of paper. The moment she opened it, she was disappointed. It certainly wasn't a map.

"It's just an old nursery rhyme!" Kate read the words to Megan:

> Young Mother Hubbard,
> Went to the cupboard,
> To get her poor friend a bone,
> But when she got there,
> The cupboard was bare,
> And so the poor friend had none.

"I remember hearing that rhyme when I was little," Megan said. "But the words aren't quite the same."

"I wonder why it's here?" Kate asked. "It's sure a strange place."

Just then Erik called. "Kate! Megan! C'mon!"

Quickly Kate put the note back and replaced the brick. Arm in arm, she and Megan hurried toward the carriage house. Her cousin's surprise was ready!

The boys had washed and polished the bicycle built for two. The tires were pumped up, the chain in place. Willie stood nearby, holding an oil can.

"Kate found something for you," Erik said when the girls reached him. He took Megan's hand, set it down on the front handlebar, then the seat.

"A bicycle?" Megan sounded puzzled, as though she wondered if this was a cruel joke.

But Erik placed her hand on the second handlebar, then the second seat.

Suddenly Megan caught on. "A bicycle for two? Really truly?" She laughed as though she couldn't believe it. "I can ride again!"

"Sit down and I'll see if the seat is the right height," Anders said gruffly. With a wrench he adjusted the second seat for Megan, then the first one for Kate.

"I haven't ridden a bicycle since before the accident," Megan said as she and Kate started out.

Erik walked on one side, Willie on the other until both girls felt sure of their balance. Then Kate steered onto a quiet street. Every now and then Megan laughed, just from the excitement she felt.

As she listened to her cousin, Kate felt good. At the same time, she kept a sharp watch. Not for anything did she want that man to find Megan again.

Only after they had ridden for some time did Kate remember they had planned to search the attic that afternoon. Soon after she and Megan returned to the carriage house all of them gathered around the supper table.

Megan turned to Kate. "I have an idea."

"For solving the mystery?" Kate asked.

Megan shook her head. "You know the talent contest I told you about? I was going to play the piano while I sang. But do you want to play for me?"

"Sure!" Kate answered. She had told Megan how much she liked the piano in the mansion.

A moment later Kate had second thoughts. "Do you really think I can do it?"

"Let's see how it goes," Megan said. "If you play for me, I need to practice walking out on the stage. You and I can go over to the opera house after supper."

"You're singing at an opera house? The one we saw?" Kate was impressed.

So was Anders. "My little sister is going to play in an *opera house*?"

Megan giggled.

"You want me to play *there*?" Kate asked.

"You can do it," Megan told her. "Let's ride the bike over."

When they reached the Red Jacket Opera House, Kate and Megan entered by the main door. Kate fumbled around until she found the light switches, then led Megan into the auditorium.

The ceiling extended far above them with lights set around a great circle. Kate stared up at the beautifully decorated arches that framed the stage.

She and Megan walked down the center aisle. From there Kate

looked back toward the balconies. It seemed as if the second balcony reached to the sky.

Megan wanted to walk onto the stage as if she could see where she was going. As Kate looked around, she studied the floor. Though laid from one side of the stage to the other, there were three places where the boards had been sawed, separating them from the rest of the floor. One of these places was a large rectangle, and the two other places were smaller rectangles. The largest rectangle provided a perfect place for Megan to stand.

"I'm not sure if you can feel this with your foot," Kate said. "Can you tell that some boards are laid in a different direction?"

The wood was so level with the floor that Megan couldn't feel the difference. Instead, she decided to count her steps from the side of the stage. Kate lined her up, and Megan walked straight to the rectangle.

"Just don't walk off the stage!" Kate warned. "It's a long drop to the floor of the auditorium!"

Kate set the music for *The Irish Lullaby* on the piano, then sat down. After playing a few lines of music, she glanced out into the auditorium. Suddenly her heart went thumpety-thump, and she stopped playing. Even the idea of performing in such a great hall was frightening.

Kate glanced toward her cousin. Megan stood almost in front of her. Not even a twinge of fear showed on Megan's face.

Trying to push aside her scared feelings, Kate started playing again. As Megan began to sing the lullaby she had chosen, her clear voice echoed in the empty auditorium.

Kate was a good sight reader but had never played the song before. Leaning forward, she concentrated totally on the music. Suddenly she heard Megan cry out.

"Kate! Help!"

Kate looked up. Megan wasn't there!

Filled with panic, Kate leaped off the piano stool. The section of floor on which Megan stood had dropped out of sight. A large square hole remained.

"Kate!" Megan cried again, and Kate ran toward the sound of her voice. As though standing in an elevator without sides, Megan was moving downward.

Kneeling on the floor, Kate peered into the dimly lighted basement. Just then she saw a hand reach out and grab Megan's arm.

Kate jumped up and stumbled away from the hole. Fear knotted her insides as she struggled to think. *Where did I see some stairs?*

At the side of the stage, she found the stairway and hurried down. When she reached the basement, she stood there, unable to believe what she saw.

"How did *you* get in?" Kate asked her brother and Erik.

"The door was unlocked," Anders answered calmly.

Still holding Megan's arm, Willie helped her climb down from where she stood. Raised and lowered with ropes and pulleys, the platform offered a way for actors and actresses to disappear during a play.

"A trapdoor?" Kate asked.

Anders grinned at Kate. "Pretty good trick, huh? Willie showed us how to work it."

But Erik looked at Kate and said, "Maybe not so good."

A surge of anger flooded Kate. "I've never been so scared in my whole life!" she exclaimed. "Megan, are you all right?"

Megan laughed. "I am now."

"You could have stepped off and fallen. There aren't any sides."

Now that her fright was over, Megan didn't seem nearly as concerned as Kate. "It was what you'd call an adventure, I guess." For some reason Megan almost seemed happy.

Kate was still angry. "You stupid boys! What are you going to try next?"

"Aw, Kate!" Anders said. "Can't you take a joke?"

Kate was in no mood for fooling around. "You get out of here! And don't you dare come back!"

Back on the stage once more, Kate again played the introduction. She heard the boys tromp through an aisle, but paid no attention. In the main part of the auditorium the lights suddenly went out.

Kate stopped playing.

"What's wrong?" Megan asked.

"They turned off the lights!"

"But not on the stage," Megan said. "I can see a crack of light. Can you see the music?"

"Yes," Kate answered. "And there's a light back next to the entrance. But everything in between is dark. All those empty seats—"

"Oh, never mind," Megan said. "I don't need the lights!"

This time it was Kate who giggled. For the third time she played the introduction. Partway through the song, Megan stopped singing while Kate played an interlude.

At the right place Megan again started singing. Moments later, she stopped. "Kate?" she asked softly.

At the look on Megan's face, Kate leaped up from the piano. She hurried over to Megan.

"What's wrong?" Kate whispered.

"I don't know." Megan looked scared. "When you were playing alone, I thought I heard a door close. Now it's like someone's watching me."

Kate glanced out over the empty seats, up to the far reaches of the second balcony. "It's too dark to see," Kate said. "But I don't think anyone's there."

"But there is," Megan said. "It's as though someone is staring at me. If he's staring at me, he's staring at you."

"He?" Kate asked.

"He—she." Megan sounded impatient. "Look again, Kate. I heard someone—somewhere out in the seats. Don't you see *anything?*"

Once again, Kate peered into the darkness. This time she caught a movement in the dim light near the entrance. The movement was so slight Kate would have missed it if she hadn't been looking. Someone had slipped down behind a seat.

Kate put her hand on Megan's shoulder and stepped close. "You're right. There's someone there." Kate hoped her voice didn't carry.

"Where?" Megan asked.

"At the back of the auditorium. Near the center doors."

"I knew it!" Megan exclaimed. "Someone followed us here—maybe that man!"

"Maybe it's the boys." Kate was whispering. "Maybe they're trying to scare us again."

"I don't think so," Megan whispered back.

As much as Kate wanted to believe her own words, she felt more like agreeing with Megan. She stared at the center door, then at the two side ones. Except for the dim light from the entrance she could see nothing.

Then she heard the floor creak. Without moving, Kate listened, heard a footstep. A heavy footstep, as if the person wore boots.

Megan stiffened. "Where can we hide?"

Grabbing Megan's hand, Kate pulled her toward the area on the right side of the stage. They had barely stepped behind the curtains when Kate heard footsteps moving closer.

Megan trembled. Frantically Kate looked around. Nearby, steps led upward. Still holding Megan's hand, Kate ran toward them and hurried up the steep flight. When they reached a door, Kate flung it open and switched on the light.

The dressing room was small, with no hiding place. Whirling around, Kate pulled Megan back down the steps. Whoever was there was closer, walking across the floor in front of the stage.

Kate's heart pounded. *Who is it?* she wondered, afraid to find out. Again she looked around.

The overhead stage lights shone between the curtains, throwing long shadows. If she and Megan went out on the stage, they'd be cut off from the main entrance. If they tried the side aisles, the man would see them and catch up. Kate had no desire to face a stranger in the big empty theater. Whoever it was couldn't be trusted, or he would have called to them.

Stepping away from Megan, Kate whirled around, searching. At the back of the stage was a large backdrop—scenery painted on heavy canvas. Next to it and far above was a high catwalk—a narrow walking place that extended from one side of the stage to the other.

Next to the catwalk and just above Kate was a wider, open platform. Only a narrow rail surrounded its sides.

"Follow me," Kate whispered as she returned to her cousin.

This time Kate drew Megan to a wooden ladder attached to the high stone wall of the opera house.

"We're going to climb." Kate set Megan's hand on a rung of the ladder.

As quickly as Kate moved, Megan followed. Higher and higher Kate went. Megan kept up with her. At last Kate stepped out onto the platform.

As Kate turned back to give Megan her hand, footsteps crossed the wooden stage below. Whoever it was, he was no longer trying to be quiet.

"Lie down," Kate whispered. Tugging Megan's hand, Kate showed her where the open platform was safe.

When Megan dropped to her stomach, Kate lay down beside her. Peering beneath the railing, Kate looked down over the edge of the platform. Just inside the range of light, Kate glimpsed a man's head.

The man was not fat, but not thin either. He was tall with light brown curly hair.

Curly! Kate thought, remembering the name of the man on the train from Wisconsin.

She ducked back, lying flat with her head against the boards of the platform. As she listened, the footsteps drew closer, then stopped.

Barely breathing, Kate lay without moving. Whoever the man was, he must be looking up.

An instant later the man moved, his footsteps echoing on the wooden stage. As though he had made up his mind, he walked toward the ladder.

Mysterious Happenings

In that moment Kate saw Megan's skirt. It hung just slightly over the edge of the platform. No doubt the man had seen it too. He knew where they were.

Her heart pounding, Kate looked down. The man was almost to the ladder. If he started up, he'd cut off their escape. Where could they go?

Then Kate remembered. On the other side of the stage, she'd seen a steel ladder. It, too, was attached to the wall. The catwalk—a narrow walkway—lay between.

Far below, the man set his foot on the ladder beneath them. Kate tugged Megan's hand.

Trying not to make a sound, Kate stood up. As Megan stood with her, Kate peered down over the railing. She caught a quick glimpse of a short-sleeved shirt—a blue shirt like the one she'd seen at Central Mine. That man had ducked behind a house as though trying to hide.

Moving as quickly as she dared, Kate led Megan across the rest of the platform to where it connected with the catwalk. Only a few feet wide, the catwalk lay in shadows. Only one board—a narrow railing—separated them from a long fall and certain death. Yet Kate started across.

Once Megan thudded against the flimsy railing. Kate's heart stopped as she clung to her cousin's hand. Only Megan's quick intake of breath told Kate that her cousin knew the danger. Yet Megan barely missed a step.

As Kate reached the end of the catwalk, she looked back. On the other side of the stage, the man stood on the platform.

"We have to go down another ladder," Kate told Megan. "You first."

Taking her cousin's hand, Kate set it on the top rung, then guided Megan's foot to a rung farther down.

"Go ahead," she said.

Megan trembled, but obeyed. As quickly as she could, she hurried down the ladder. Kate followed, her own feet nearly stepping on Megan's hands.

When they reached the floor of the stage, Kate took the lead again. Together they ran through the auditorium. At the front entrance Kate tore open the door, then slammed it shut behind them.

"The police!" Kate was panting now. "Somewhere I saw a police station. Where was it?"

"We're on the front side?" Megan asked. "Then it's around the corner from here. At least that's where it used to be. In the same building, but around the corner."

As they left the main entrance of the opera house behind, they passed another door, then rounded the corner of the building. Not far beyond was the police station. Flinging wide the door, Kate tumbled inside with Megan right behind.

Kate poured out the story to Sergeant Maki, the police officer on duty.

"I'll look," the sergeant said. The girls followed him back to the opera house.

Sergeant Maki searched from top to bottom, even walking into the first and second balconies. Finally he shook his head.

"Whoever it was must have slipped out a door when you came for me. I'm afraid he's gotten away."

Kate was afraid of the same thing. Now that it was all over, the awfulness of what had happened struck her. It was no different for Megan. As if she were freezing cold, Megan hugged herself. But her arms were shaking.

"Do you want to practice anymore?" the policeman asked. "If you do, I'll wait."

Megan shook her head.

"We better go," Kate said. She just wanted to be home.

"I'll see that you get there," the policeman said as they came out on the sidewalk.

"We have a bicycle," Kate answered.

For the first time since her scare, Megan smiled. "A bicycle built for two."

It took only a moment to return to the station for Officer Maki's horse. As the girls rode their bicycle, he stayed near them. When the girls started up the steps to the apartment in the carriage house, Kate waved to the policeman. Only when they reached the door did he leave.

Inside, the rooms were hot and empty. Kate's long braid felt warm against her back. She and Megan went back outside and sat down on the wide landing at the top of the steps.

This time the moonlight lit her cousin's face. In spite of her fright at the theater, Megan's lips looked softer, as though more ready to smile.

Her voice was softer, too, as she told Kate what Willie had said the night before. "I never dreamed he thought the accident was his fault," Megan said. "He felt so guilty it must have been even worse than being blind. He was crabby all the time. Then he'd apologize. The next minute he'd be an old crab again."

Kate had already seen the difference in Willie. "But he's still a big tease," Kate said, thinking about the trapdoor in the opera house.

"He's back to normal," Megan said. "That's the old Willie, the Willie that always figured out a way to have fun. I'm glad."

* * * * *

When Anders and Erik and Willie came home, they, too, sat down on the carriage house steps. By now a cloud covered the moon.

"At first we thought it was you again," Kate said when she told the boys what had happened.

"I'm sorry, Kate." Erik sounded worried. "We shouldn't have left you and Megan alone."

"I've always felt safe in Red Jacket and Laurium," Megan answered. "Till the last few days, that is."

"There's something I can't figure out," Kate said. "That man must be Curly. Why do you think he follows us around?"

For a moment she was silent, thinking about it. "Do you suppose he thinks we have the map? If he does, why doesn't he just wait for us to lead him to the treasure?"

As Kate looked toward the mansion, more dark clouds rolled into the area. She remembered Mr. Mitchell's request.

"We promised we'd walk through the house every once in a while," she said. "If we're going to make it look as though they're home, we better do it now." Just the same, Kate dreaded going into another dark building.

"Let's search the attic at the same time," Anders said.

"It's full of stuff," Megan answered. "Tisha has me take things there."

Willie started down the carriage house stairs. "I have to water the horses. I'll catch up."

As the rest of them stepped inside the back door of the mansion, Erik looked around for a light switch. He found a brass plate with two buttons, one above the other. When he pushed one of the buttons, the lights turned on.

Because they had only kerosene lamps at Windy Hill Farm, Kate still wasn't used to such a luxury. It was fun going around, putting on lights in the first and second floor. Then she and Megan followed the boys to the back of the house. Next to the servants' stairway another set of steps led to the attic.

Here the light switch was mounted on a porcelain base. A black knob stuck out from the center of the nickel-plated cover. When Erik turned the knob to the right, the light turned on with a loud click.

They found the huge attic filled with boxes and old furniture.

"We could look for a month and not find something up here!" Anders exclaimed.

Just the same, they decided to try. They divided into teams, with Erik and Kate working together and Anders guiding Megan.

It wasn't long before Kate's hands were gray with dirt. In spite of the windows Erik opened, the attic was very hot. Yet they all worked on, opening boxes and peering into old drawers. Whenever Megan came to a piece of furniture, she tapped the wood, listening for something hollow.

"You know," Kate said finally, "we're going at this the wrong way. We should try the very back of the attic first. Wouldn't the oldest stuff be there?"

"Good idea!" Erik answered. "See that desk in the farthest corner? It looks like it's been there forever."

"What could be a better hiding place?" Once again excited about searching, Kate started toward the desk. Partway there, she turned on another light. Again the switch made a loud click.

When Megan put her hand on his shoulder, she and Anders followed Kate and Erik to the far side of the attic. Thunder rumbled in the distance.

In spite of the heat, Kate shivered. The big boxes around her offered a hundred hiding places. *I wouldn't want to be caught here in the dark!* she thought.

A moment later the attic lights went out.

Kate's Discovery

In the darkness Kate heard a quick movement, then footsteps running across the floor.

"Erik?" Kate asked. All her earlier fear came back.

"I'm here," he said, taking her arm.

In a minute Kate caught the dim glow of the streetlight, reflecting up through a window. At least it gave a sense of direction.

"I've got the light," Anders said. Several times Kate heard a loud click, but nothing happened.

"Someone got past us!" Erik exclaimed.

"Megan?" Kate asked and found her cousin's hand.

Together they stumbled around boxes to reach the stairway. When they started down the steps, not even one window gave them light.

Megan took the lead. Forming a chain, the others followed her down the stairs. On the second floor the lights they had turned on were out. Megan led them down the servants' stairway to the ground floor, which was also dark.

The back door was closed as they had left it. Megan found her way through the dark rooms, and the others followed.

When they reached the front door, Kate took one look and knew they were too late. A crack of light showed where the door was not fully closed.

Outside, the four circled the mansion, looking for someone. Near the stable they found Willie.

"So it was you in the attic!" Kate exclaimed.

"Me? What are you talking about?"

"Creeping around up there. Turning off the lights. Running out ahead of us!"

"Not me!" Willie answered. "I've been here ever since I left you."

"William Henry Pascoe!" Kate was tired and hot, worn out by all that had happened that evening. "Stop playing games!"

"Kate——" Megan said.

But Kate was upset now, as angry as she had been in the opera house. "I am *so* tired of the tricks you boys play. It's rotten enough without you lying!"

"Kate——" Megan tried again. "It wasn't Willie in the attic."

Kate whirled around. "You're sure?"

"It wasn't his footsteps," Megan said.

"Sorry, Willie." Kate explained what had happened.

"All the lights are out?" Willie asked. "That's strange. They're not out in the stable or across the street. So it's only the mansion where something's wrong."

"Whatever happened, I didn't hear a loud click when the lights went out," Kate said.

"Then I know what's wrong!" Willie answered. "The electric wire comes in at the attic. There's a breaker switch there that turns all the lights on or off."

"You're sure?" Erik asked.

Willie nodded. "I've watched Pa a hundred times. If something goes wrong at home, he stands on the top of a stepladder and pulls himself through a hole in the ceiling. It's a lot of work to fix things."

"In the mansion there's a stairway to the attic," Megan told him.

In that instant Kate had an awful thought. "Maybe someone shut off the electricity so they could rob the house!"

She flipped her braid over her shoulders. "*That's* what we're supposed to keep from happening!"

As they hurried back to the mansion, thunder rumbled again, moving closer. With Kate holding a candle, they climbed the stairs to the attic. When Willie turned the breaker switch, the lights flooded on.

Together they hurried down to the second floor. Here, too, the lights were on. It gave Kate a creepy feeling.

"I don't like it," she said. "Whoever was in this house didn't want to take a chance on being seen."

They decided to search the mansion again, looking for anything that seemed different. Staying together, they walked rapidly through the house, searching room by room. On the second floor and most of the main floor, things seemed just the same.

Then in the parlor Megan sniffed. "Are those roses still here?" she asked.

Kate looked around. "What roses?"

"The ones Tisha put here on Monday."

Then Kate remembered. She had seen Tisha bring in vases filled with red roses. "They're gone now," Kate said.

"But the scent is still here," her cousin answered.

Kate sniffed. Now that Megan mentioned it, Kate also noticed the scent. "How long would the smell stay in the air?" she asked.

Megan shrugged. "Tisha never lets roses get old. She doesn't want petals to fall on the tables. Usually she throws out the flowers, then opens all the windows."

"But we can smell them two days later," Kate said. "If Tisha threw out the flowers before she went, where would she put them?"

"There's a trash basket in a closet off the kitchen," Megan answered and led Kate there.

Kate found the basket filled with flowers. They looked as if they had been quickly tossed aside. A few of the roses had spilled onto the floor.

Kate told her cousin, and Megan shook her head. "That's not like Tisha."

When Kate and Megan returned to the front of the house, they found the three boys standing in the entry. Turning around, Kate looked up the beautiful stairway leading off the wide hall.

"While we went down the back steps, the person in the attic used these!" she said.

As Kate spoke, thunder rumbled again, this time from close at hand.

"I have to get home," Willie said. "Pa will wonder where I am."

As soon as he left, Kate and the others locked up the mansion. As they walked over to the carriage house, a jagged bolt of lightning streaked across the sky.

By now Megan's parents had returned. As soon as Casey heard all that had happened, he hurried away to talk with Sergeant Maki.

"I'll make popcorn," Megan said when Breda went to bed. In the woodbox Megan found poplar for a fire that would burn quickly, then go out.

When the fire was hot, Megan put butter and popcorn into a kettle, covered it, and pushed the kettle back and forth across the hottest part of the cookstove. When the corn stopped popping, Megan poured it out into a bowl.

"There's plenty of milk." She set four glasses and a pitcher on the kitchen table.

As they gathered around the bowl of popcorn, large drops of rain splatted against the landing outside the door.

"There's something we need to figure out," Kate said. "Were the roses in the parlor when we searched the mansion yesterday?"

No one could remember.

Erik had another question. "Who was in the mansion and why?"

"Whoever it is, he's trying to beat us to the treasure map," Anders said.

"Megan," Kate asked, "did the footsteps in the opera house and the ones in the attic sound the same?"

Without giving it a second thought, Megan shook her head. "No, Kate, they didn't."

A fist seemed to close around Kate's heart. "So there are two different people. That fits with what I heard on the train coming from Wisconsin."

The idea bothered her. It might be harder to catch two people. It also seemed to make everything more dangerous.

"But if there are two different people—" Kate was thinking aloud. "The man at the store tried to talk to you, Megan. Maybe that's the same man who followed us in the opera house. But the person in the attic ran away. Why?"

Kate took a handful of popcorn. "What was it that the man at the store said to you, Megan?"

" 'I wanna know what you found out.' "

"Maybe he'd been drinking just enough so he talked more than he usually would," Erik said.

"Or maybe—" Kate was still thinking. "Maybe the two crooks don't trust each other. Maybe Curly is trying to beat the other crook to the treasure!"

Moments later, the wind struck the trees outside the carriage house. Windows rattled as sheets of rain pounded against them.

"I hope Daddy's not out in this," Megan said.

"I hope so too," Kate answered. When she was a child, her Daddy O'Connell had drawn her into his arms when it stormed. Together they had watched lightning and listened to thunder. Because of that memory, Kate had liked thunderstorms. More recently, she had also learned to respect them.

Thunder rumbled, then cracked close at hand. As Anders reached for more popcorn, he knocked over his glass. Spilled milk ran across the table.

Kate grabbed a wet cloth and started wiping up. "Nice wood," she told Megan.

Here and there were a few nicks and the eight-sided pedestal leg looked worn. Yet the table was still beautiful.

"Ma says it came from the mansion."

"It did?" Kate asked, instantly alert. "When?"

Megan shrugged. "Before we came here. Maybe when Mrs. Mitchell redecorated."

Kate ran the cloth along the center crack, trying to get all of the milk. Some had dripped down between the two halves of the table. With the heat they'd been having, the milk would soon sour.

"Let's pull the table apart," Kate said.

Megan held one side while Kate tugged on the other. Only a narrow crack appeared.

The two halves seemed stuck, as though it had been a long time since the table was opened. Kate leaned across. "Pull it more," she said.

It took Erik on one side and Anders on the other to open the table as far as it could go. Now Kate got a good look down inside the center leg.

Filled with excitement, she laughed. "I thought so! The leg is hollow!"

Suddenly she reached down. At the very bottom of the hollow, she felt a piece of paper. Carefully she brought it up.

The paper was folded in half. Kate hardly dared breathe. With trembling fingers she opened it.

"It's a map!" Kate squealed. "We found it!"

Erik and Anders jumped up to see.

"Look at the way it's drawn!" Erik said. "The writing is old and spidery looking."

"Maybe the person who drew it was sick." Kate took a better look. "Or in a big hurry."

The map showed a pointing finger of land that reached out into Lake Superior. Clearly the land was an outline of the Keweenaw Peninsula. Many of the Copper Country villages and cities were marked—Hancock and Houghton, Red Jacket, Laurium, Eagle Harbor, Copper Harbor, and Fort Wilkins.

Then the person who drew the map started using initials instead of names. Two A's stood close together, then a C, a P, another C, and a D.

Down in the corner on the right hand side of the map were instructions:

> When A plus M
> plus C and P
> equal C minus D,
> you'll find the treasure house.
> Nearby you'll find another treasure.
> Watch where the apples fall.

Erik stared at the map. "It doesn't seem quite right," he said.

"Don't forget that the Keweenaw Central Railroad is new," Megan reminded him.

"That explains it." A crash of thunder muffled Erik's voice.

Suddenly Megan stiffened. "There's someone at the door."

15

Megan's Contest

Kate whirled around. The glass in the door was dark with night, empty even of shadows. Kate tried to laugh. "Megan, you're getting jumpy."

"No one would be out in this storm," Anders told her.

"I think it's thunder you're hearing," Erik said.

"I think you're all wrong," Megan answered. "There's someone there."

As Megan started toward the door, Kate caught a better look at her face. Megan was worried again, even scared.

Kate hurried to the door with her. Outside, the wind still tossed tree branches up and down. The mansion blocked the light from the street corner.

Just to be sure, Kate stepped onto the landing and looked around. Darkness and rain made it difficult to see. In two seconds Kate was wet, but found nothing.

"You've always been right," she told Megan. "But if someone was there, he's gone."

"He went down the steps," Megan answered.

Kate felt uneasy. She tried to tell herself that they would have noticed someone looking through the glass in the door. Yet thunder still rumbled in the distance. Someone could have walked up and down the steps without their knowing.

When Kate returned to the table, she and Anders and Erik studied every detail of the map. The instructions at the bottom seemed confusing.

"Do you have a map of the Keweenaw?" Kate asked her cousin.

Megan's map was wooden with a wide groove outlining the Keweenaw Peninsula, separating it from Lake Superior. Brass tacks and Braille symbols marked mining villages and cities.

The initials on the treasure map were in the same location as the brass tacks. Using the tips of her fingers, Megan read her map.

"Here's Allouez and Ahmeek," she said. Her fingers moved toward the point of the peninsula. "Mohawk, then Cliff and Phoenix."

"All riiiiight!" Anders exclaimed. He was following the words at the bottom of the treasure map. "When Allouez or Ahmeek—the A could be either one of them—plus Mohawk, plus Cliff and Phoenix! What are the next towns?"

Again Megan read with her fingers. "Central, then Delaware."

" 'C minus D!' It's Central we want!" Anders exclaimed. "That fits with what Willie told us. Let's go back to Central tomorrow!"

Much as she wanted to find the treasure, Kate shook her head. "We better go Friday. Megan's contest is tomorrow night. We can't take a chance on not getting back in time."

"There's something else," Erik said. "We can't forget there's a man following us. Somehow we've got to get the treasure without him knowing it."

"Mr. Mitchell comes back on Sunday," Megan said. "If we find the treasure on Friday, we'll have it for him."

Anders grinned. "Just so we get it before we go home Monday. Without us, that treasure will be lost forever!"

They decided that the safest place for the map would be where it had been hidden through the years. Kate put the map at the bottom of the hollow center leg. The boys pushed the two halves of the table back together.

On Thursday morning, Kate felt nervous just thinking about the talent contest that night. *Can I really play well enough for Megan?* she asked herself more than once.

It worried Kate. She didn't want to spoil her cousin's singing. More than once, though, Megan told Kate she would do just great. Megan didn't seem to have a nervous bone in her body.

After an early supper, Megan brushed her hair till it shone, then pulled it back in one long braid. Kate put on her white dress, and Megan wore one that brought out the blue of her eyes.

"You look beautiful, Megan," Kate said.

A soft flush colored Megan's cheeks. "Thanks, Kate. I'm sure you look nice too."

"I wish you could see yourself," Kate answered.

"So do I. But when you tell me, I know."

"Megan, how do you do it?" Kate asked suddenly. They were alone in Megan's room, and Kate knew her cousin would be honest.

"Do what?"

"Be the way you are."

Megan sat down on the bed next to Kate. "I still get really mad at myself—at everyone. I still get upset about things."

"Like what?" Kate asked. Though a few months younger than Kate, Megan seemed older. "Besides Willie, I mean."

"Last week I walked into a tree. I pounded that stupid old tree with my fists."

Kate laughed. It was exactly the kind of thing she herself would do. But then she felt sorry for laughing. "It isn't funny, is it?"

"C & H has a broom factory," Megan answered. "Blind men work there—men who can't see because of a mining accident. After my accident, when I was really mad at God, one of those men came to talk to me."

Megan grinned. "If it had been anyone else, I'd have told him he didn't know what he was talking about. But he treated me like a grown-up. He answered questions I didn't know I had. He even said, 'You know, Megan, you did something that wasn't very smart.'

"I wanted to die, right there. But then he said, 'You fell, and that's what can happen if someone stands up in a moving wagon.'"

Megan drew a deep breath. "I'll never forget his words, Kate. He said, 'God wasn't trying to be mean. If you stay mad at God, you won't let Him help you. You won't let Him be your friend.'"

Megan's lips quivered, but she tried to smile. "God's my friend now, Kate. I'm glad that He's also yours."

* * * * *

When they reached the Red Jacket Opera House, Kate felt as nervous as the cat in Mr. Mitchell's stable. She and Megan waited backstage with the other people in the talent contest.

By the time Megan listened to several other performers, she had a bad case of stage fright. "Will you pray for me, Kate?" she asked. "I'm so scared I won't be able to sing!"

As Kate prayed silently, she remembered how scared she'd been the first time she played in front of Erik.

"My organ teacher taught me something," Kate said. "He asked me to pick out someone in the audience who believed in me. He told me to smile at that person before I started playing."

"I'll pretend I'm seeing Ma," Megan said. "And Daddy, too. I'm glad he can be here tonight."

When it came time to go on, Kate faced Megan in the right direction. "Walk straight ahead," Kate reminded her. "Then make a right turn. You'll be facing the audience."

As soon as Megan was announced, she walked out. As Kate took her seat on the piano bench, Megan made her right turn.

Her hands above the keyboard, Kate waited. As though she saw her parents in the audience, Megan smiled. Kate played the introduction to *The Irish Lullaby*, and Megan began singing. As she reached the chorus, the notes fell clear and sweet upon the audience.

> "Tu ra lu ra lu ra,
> Tu ra lu ra lay—"

All through the song, Kate concentrated on playing, but she knew something special was happening. When the last note died away, the entire hall remained silent, as if people could not move.

Megan looked puzzled, as though wondering if she had done something wrong. Then a man blew his nose. Several people coughed. From somewhere in the middle of the audience, a person clapped.

Immediately everyone else joined in. A young man leaped to his feet. The rest of the audience followed in a standing ovation.

"More! More!" they cried out, clapping as hard as they could. Near the back, someone started stamping his feet. Others joined him, and the sound moved forward, like waves on a beach.

As though unsure what to do, Megan turned toward Kate. But the woman in charge of the contest reached Megan.

"As you can hear, we'd like to keep clapping forever," she told Megan. "Will you sing the song again for us?"

At the end of the show, Megan won first place. As she walked out on the stage, Kate knew that Megan was counting her steps. Standing off to the side, Kate felt as if she would burst with pride.

The woman presenting the awards reached out, took Megan's hand, and congratulated her. "You've won the highest honor we have to give!"

Megan's face shone as she received the framed certificate and four free tickets to a play. Again the audience stomped and cheered.

Megan took her bows, then hesitated. As the woman called the second-place winner, Megan turned the wrong way.

Kate's heart thudded. If her cousin walked straight, she'd reach the opposite side of the stage. If she didn't, she'd walk right off the edge!

Kate dropped behind the back curtain, broke into a run. Racing around the stage, she reached the other side. As Kate looked out, Megan stopped, as if she knew something was wrong.

"Megan!" Kate called in a stage whisper.

Megan smiled and walked straight toward Kate's voice.

Outside the Red Jacket Opera House, Kate and Megan waited with the others while one carriage after another pulled up. When Casey finally arrived, Kate nearly leaped from the sidewalk.

"Megan, your daddy brought the best carriage!"

"In honor of me darlin'!" Breda said. After the performance she had surrounded Megan with a big hug. But Kate knew Breda was holding back her tears.

It was Willie who helped Megan into the carriage, as if he escorted ladies every day of his life. When Anders was going to help Kate, Erik beat him to it.

As Casey flicked the reins over the horses, Kate looked back toward the opera house entrance. In that instant a cold blue gaze met hers.

Kate stiffened. *Am I imagining things?*

Then the carriage moved forward. Kate poked Erik. "There. Under the roof over the entrance. Next to the door. Do you see Tisha?"

Erik stared in that direction. If Tisha was there, the crowd had closed around her.

"I'm sure it was her!" Kate said.

"If it was, it's mighty strange."

"*Real* strange," Kate answered. "Willie took her to the depot. She's not supposed to be in town."

The whole idea upset Kate, but she tried to push it aside. She didn't want to spoil Megan's evening.

Erik leaned closer, spoke softly. "You know, you played really well."

"You think so?"

"You didn't miss a note. And you were with her—really with her."

"I wanted to play well for Megan's sake."

"You did. I was proud of you."

Pure joy welled up inside Kate. She tried to say thanks, to smile at Erik, but she couldn't utter a word.

Casey took them for a ride around Red Jacket and Laurium. By the time they reached home, a light breeze had cooled down the July evening. The air was sweet with the scent of flowers. Kate felt as if she would never forget that night.

When Casey dropped them off at the carriage house, Kate was the first one up the steps. At the landing she almost stepped on something.

Bending down, she picked up a rose that had been placed there, along with a paper.

"Someone's congratulating you already," she called down to Megan.

As soon as Breda opened the door, Kate carried the paper to a light. When she read the words, her knees felt weak.

> Roses are red,
> Violets are blue.
> Someone's too snoopy,
> I think it's you.

"What have you got, Kate?" Erik asked.

"Don't show it to Megan," Kate whispered. "Don't spoil her evening."

But Megan heard Kate talking. "Don't show me what?"

16

Hornets!

"Why is someone warning us off?" Kate asked when they explained to Megan. "Up till now Curly *wanted* us to find the treasure!"

The whole thing really bothered Kate. Long after she went to bed, she could not sleep. Questions kept going round and round in her head.

During the night she heard Casey return to the apartment. A long time later, she heard him leave again. Though he would be out of town on Mr. Mitchell's business for only two days, Kate wished Casey could stay home. What if something more happened?

In the darkness before dawn, Kate remembered the message hidden beneath the brick. At the time she found it, the words hadn't seemed important. Now Kate wondered if the handwriting on the two messages was the same.

Soon after the sun edged up over the horizon, she hurried over to the mansion. When she removed the brick, Kate found a piece of paper. The handwriting was different from the note of the night before. To Kate's surprise the message was also different. Someone had changed the first note she had found for a new one:

> Jack Sprat could eat no fat,
> His wife could eat no lean,
> And so between the two of them,
> They licked the table clean.

" 'Licked the *table* clean?' Oh no!"

Quickly Kate replaced the message and the brick. Whirling around, she ran for the carriage house. When she reached the kitchen, she found Breda making breakfast.

"Help me pull the table apart!" Kate said.

As she had feared, the treasure map was gone. Kate woke up Megan, then the boys, telling them the bad news. In spite of the early hour, they were all wide awake when they gathered around the table with Breda.

Anders groaned. "Megan, you were right after all. There *was* someone on the steps—someone who looked in that window!"

"But who?" Kate felt sick inside. "Do you think it was Curly?" After being so close to the treasure, they had missed their big opportunity.

"The map was stolen while we were gone last night," Erik said. "That crook knows every move we make! But why does he leave nursery rhymes around? It's like some strange code or something."

"Code!" Kate exclaimed. "That's it! Remember those two people on the train from Wisconsin? One of them said, 'If you leave a message, make sure it's in our secret code'!"

To make matters worse, Kate and the boys had only three days before they needed to leave for home. As they talked about what to do, Breda looked worried. "I wish your daddy was here, Megan. He always has good ideas!"

But Kate was still thinking. Slowly she repeated the words of the first message she found beneath the brick. "*Young* Mother Hubbard, not *old*. Yet the cupboard was *bare*."

In that moment Kate understood. "The person who left that message was telling the other crook he didn't find anything!"

"But now he did!" Erik said. "He got the map from the table!"

"If only I had caught on before!" Kate answered. "If we know the nursery rhyme and see which words are changed, we might understand what the code says!"

They decided that whoever stole the map would be looking around Central Mine that day.

"We'll have to beat him to the treasure!" Anders said. "If we don't, it'll be gone for good!"

When they told Willie what had happened, he wanted to go with them. While Breda and Megan packed a lunch, Kate, Anders, and Eriks wrote down what they remembered from the map.

"I think that's it," Kate said finally.

Once again they took the streetcar, then the train to Central Mine. All the way there, they talked about where to search.

"What's the treasure house?" Kate asked. "The church, do you think?"

Willie thought it might be the shaft house because of the copper-bearing rock that came up.

"How about the school?" Megan asked.

When they reached Central, they went to the church, then the shaft-house. When they couldn't find anything at either place, they climbed the hill to the schoolhouse. Again nothing seemed out of the ordinary.

Already the sun was high in the sky and starting to slip westward. "If we aren't careful, we'll run out of time," Megan warned. "We can't miss the last train to Red Jacket."

"What do we do now?" Willie asked as they all sat down on the edge of the bluff.

The July heat beat down upon them. Each time Kate swung her head, her braid felt heavier. There had to be something they were missing. What was it?

"Watch where the apples fall," Kate said. "That's close to a tree." Yet as she looked down over the town, there were a great number of houses with apple trees.

"There's something we're doing wrong," Kate said. "Let's think back. When the miner named Ellis found the silver, he hid it. He suddenly needed to see his sick brother and borrowed more money from Mr. Mitchell's father. He said, 'Use this map if I don't come back.' Mr. Mitchell had been kind to him. If Ellis was honest, he wouldn't make it impossible for Mr. Mitchell to find the treasure."

They decided to walk from one end of the town to the other, looking at any place where they found an apple tree. After dividing up the streets, Anders and Erik went one direction, and Kate, Megan, and Willie another.

They had searched a number of streets when Willie suddenly stopped dead in his tracks.

"How stupid can I be?" he asked. "The treasure house. The pay office! Why didn't I think of that before?"

Willie led Kate and Megan to the building where the miners had received pay for their work. At the front of the building, there was no apple tree. But when they walked around to the back, they discovered a path overgrown with weeds.

Along the path, water running down the hill had created washouts. Rocks, steel rods, and pieces of old track lay beneath the weeds. Kate tried to guide Megan around the trash, but she stumbled twice.

Finally Megan said, "I'm slowing you down, and we don't have much time left. I'll just wait here."

"I don't want to leave you," Kate said.

But Megan insisted. "Go on. I'll be fine."

Trees and bushes had grown up on either side of the path. Megan sat down in the shade of some tall bushes, and Kate and Willie hurried on.

They were out of sight of Megan when Kate saw an old shed. Next to it stood an apple tree with wide, spreading branches.

With growing excitement Kate stared at the shed. "Look at that tree!"

"That's a really old building!" Willie answered. "Even when the mine was open, it couldn't have been used for much!"

The boards were weather-beaten, and a door hinge was loose. Through a dirty window, Kate peered into the shed. A pick with a broken handle lay on the dirt floor. A rusty shovel rested against one wall, next to a number of kegs.

"Lime kegs!" Willie said as he gazed over Kate's shoulder.

Most of the kegs were empty, but two still had covers and looked like nail kegs. Gray with dirt, they seemed to have been there for a long time.

When Willie tried one of the double doors, it seemed stuck. After three or four tries, he took hold with both hands and pulled hard. Suddenly the door flew open.

Kate was first into the shed. In that instant she heard buzzing. Whirling around, she looked up. "Willie!" she cried. "There's hornets in here!"

Above the doorway was a broken nest, split apart when the door opened. Angry hornets spilled out.

Willie backed outside, safely away. Between Kate and the door, the hornets flew in bigger and bigger circles. Kate's heart lurched, just thinking about their sting.

Frantically she stared at them, trying to remember what she knew about bees. Would the same thing work? Somehow she had to get through.

Dropping down, Kate moved slowly, trying not to attract the hornets' attention. On her hands and knees she crawled beneath their flight path. As their angry buzzing increased, she nearly panicked. Praying the whole way, she finally reached the outdoors.

Her dress was filthy and her knees full of stones when she finally dared to stand up. Two hornets had followed her. Still being careful to move quietly, Kate finally left them behind.

When she caught up with Willie, they started running. More than once Kate stumbled and nearly fell in the weed-covered path. But when they came to Megan, Kate forgot the hornets.

Her cousin stood in long grass, looking as though she wanted to run but unsure where to go. She seemed even more upset than on the day she walked to the store.

"That man is here!" Megan's face was white, and her voice trembled.

"Here?" Kate asked. "How do you know?"

"I smelled him," Megan said. "I was sitting by the bushes, and I smelled him!"

Kate glanced toward the bushes. They offered a thick cover for anyone who wanted to hide.

"He had been drinking?"

Megan shook her head. "It was that other smell. I don't know what it is. But it was the man who stopped me at the store."

Daddy's Gone A-Hunting

Just then the train whistle sounded. Like it or not, there was no more time to search that day.

"Come on, Meg," Willie said. Taking her hand, he guided Megan back to the road. Once they reached smoother ground, Megan put her hand on Willie's shoulder. The three hurried toward the street leading down the hill. There they met Anders and Erik.

With Willie still guiding Megan, they ran the rest of the way to catch the train before it left.

As they climbed aboard, Kate saw that her dress was filthy. She felt hot and discouraged, and the others looked the same way.

Though away from the deserted path, Megan still seemed scared. "Is there something men use that smells good but isn't perfume?" she asked on the way back to Red Jacket.

"Sure thing!" Anders said. "Guys put stuff on their hair to slick it down. Is that what you mean?"

"I think so. It's a smell I probably should like, but I don't because it makes me think about that man."

"He must have been there, looking around." Anders sounded angry.

"That shack we found—" Kate looked at Willie. "It seemed to fit better than any place we saw." She told the others about the hornets.

"There's one good thing," Erik said. "If it's full of hornets, that crook can't go in there either. Not unless he doesn't care about getting stung."

"Maybe the hornets will settle down overnight," Kate said. "Let's go back tomorrow."

That evening Kate and Anders, Megan and Erik once again walked around inside the mansion. Turning on lights, they made it look as if the Mitchells were home. Nothing seemed unusual or out of place.

As they left the house, Kate checked the loose brick. This time the space was empty. Without doubt, two people were using the hiding place to pass messages.

On her way back to the carriage house, Kate thought about it. That side of the mansion was close to the street. Anyone walking by could easily leave a message. That person could be Curly. But who was receiving the messages?

"If we read the notes before they're picked up, we'll know what the crooks are thinking!" Kate told the others.

Early the next morning, she hurried back to the mansion. No new message had been hidden during the night. Again the hollow space was empty.

After breakfast all of them took the train to Central Mine. As soon as they got off, they headed straight for the deserted shack.

Willie and Megan stayed back while Kate, Anders, and Erik crept forward. The hornets had settled down and were rebuilding their broken nest.

But Kate took one look inside the shed and knew they were too late. The two kegs she had wanted to check were gone! Two round spots in the dirt floor showed where they had stood.

Kate groaned. "Curly beat us to it!"

Anders was looking at the marks in the dirt. "Whatever is inside those kegs is mighty heavy!"

"That could mean it's the silver nuggets!" Erik said.

The man had tipped over each keg to roll it on its side. The roll marks led out the door.

Kate was still trying to figure it out. "The crook followed us here yesterday, do you think? Stayed all night?"

A line in the long grass showed where the kegs had been rolled to the road, then lifted onto a wagon. As they followed the wagon tracks down the hill, Kate felt sick. After all their hard work, they had lost the treasure.

"Did someone come here, carrying some kegs?" Anders asked the man at the depot.

"Yup!"

"Light brown curly hair?" Anders asked.

"Yup!"

"He went on the train?"

"Yup! Bought a ticket for Red Jacket. Looked all wore out—like he'd been up all night. Too wore out to lift the kegs by himself."

"Very long ago?"

"Yup! First train to Red Jacket this morning. Friend of yours?"

"Nope!" Anders followed Kate to a wooden bench where they could wait for the next train.

"I can't believe it!" Anders complained. "We missed that guy by one train ride!"

"Yup!" Erik sat down on the other side of Kate.

Anders looked as upset as Kate felt. "Well, Curly sure had a busy night!"

"Yup!" Erik said again.

Anders reached around Kate, clapped Erik on the back. "Got any other words in you?"

"Yup! Yup!" Erik said.

In spite of how awful she felt, Kate giggled.

"That a girl!" Erik laughed.

Kate felt grateful. Somehow Erik always managed to make her feel better.

After what seemed a long wait, the next train to Red Jacket arrived. When they reached the Copper Range Depot, the boys found some men who looked as though they had been standing around for a while.

"Did a man with a couple of kegs get off the last train?" Anders asked.

The third man they talked to was able to help them. "Not two kegs," he said. "Four."

"Four?" Anders looked puzzled. "You're sure it was *four* kegs?"

"Saw him with my own eyes. Four nail kegs. He hired horses and a wagon from a livery stable. Loaded the kegs on the wagon and drove off."

"Do you know where he was going?" Kate asked quickly.

"Sure thing. Told me himself. Said, 'I got to get these over to Osceola Number 3.' "

"What did the man look like?" Anders asked.

"Brown mustache, curly hair. About your height. Not fat. Not thin. Looked strong, but he wasn't. Kegs were heavy for him."

"Do you know his name?" Anders asked.

The man shook his head, hurried on.

"He's talking about the Osceola Consolidated Mine," Willie said. "It's not far from Laurium."

"How could two kegs suddenly become four?" Kate asked.

"Silver is heavy," Willie answered. "The crook probably divided it to make the kegs lighter."

Erik was searching the ground. "Look here!" he exclaimed.

He had found a wagon track where the back right wheel showed an unusual mark on the edge of the rim. Each time the wheel passed around, the mark appeared again.

"We just have to follow that wagon track!" Erik said.

Willie reached out for Megan's hand. All of them took the streetcar, then walked quickly to the mansion. As the boys harnessed a team of horses, Kate ran over to the secret hiding place.

This time there were two rhymes instead of one. The words were scrawled, as if written in a hurry. Kate stared down at the first message:

> Jack was nimble,
> Jack was quick,
> Jack stumbled over
> the candlestick.

Kate didn't understand what the words meant. But the second note gave her the answer she needed:

> Baa, baa, black sheep,
> Have you any wool?
> Yes, sir, yes, sir,
> Four kegs full.

Four kegs! We've got the right number for sure! Kate slipped the messages back under the brick.

As soon as the buggy was ready, Anders climbed into the front seat next to Willie. Kate and Megan took the second seat, and Erik the third. On their way to the Osceola Mine, Kate told the others what she had found.

"That's me!" Willie said when Kate repeated the Jack Be Nimble rhyme. "I'm Jack!"

Kate didn't understand.

"I'm Cornish!" Willie explained. "Back in the old days, there were lots of miners named John—Jack, as people called them. There were also a lot of men needing work. When there was a job open, a Cornish miner would say, 'My Cousin Jack can do it!' Soon Jack showed up and got the job."

As Willie drove to Osceola Mine Number 3, he explained more. "If I stumbled over the candlestick, I must have stumbled onto the silver hidden at Central. It has to be those kegs we saw!"

Outside the Osceola Mine Anders noticed wagon tracks at one side of the road. The mark from the back right wheel matched what they had seen at the depot.

At the shafthouse Willie climbed down to talk to a man. Kate followed.

"Did someone come here with nail kegs?" Willie asked.

"This morning," the man told him.

"You know his name?" Willie asked.

The man shook his head. "He's surface crew. Haven't seen him before."

"But he delivered kegs?"

This time the man nodded. "About the time the day shift came on."

"I need to take a look—make sure those kegs got down in the mine," Willie said.

"Sorry, son. I can't let anyone down who doesn't work here."

"My uncle works here."

"Sure, sure. Everybody's got someone working in one mine or another."

"I mean it." Willie leaned forward. "He's boss for the day shift."

"Your uncle's name?" The man looked skeptical.

"Thomas Pascoe."

The man straightened, looked alert. "Only one problem. Everybody knows who Thomas Pascoe is. How do I know you're not just using his name?"

"You're right," Willie said suddenly, as though changing his mind.

His tone of voice surprised Kate. Only a few days before, Willie would have tried to bully the man.

"Tell you what," Willie went on. "I'll talk to my uncle when he gets off work. He'll help me out."

"Thanks, son. That's a good idea."

As Willie and Kate started back to the wagon, she noticed a piece of paper on the ground. Lodged against a fence post, the paper was crumpled as though thrown away.

Kate felt silly picking it up. Just the same, she took it along.

As the horses trotted away from the mine, Kate looked down at the paper. It was so dirty she hated to touch it. Raising her hand, she almost threw it away. At the last moment, she opened it instead.

Kate read the words:

Bye, bye, baby bunting,
Daddy's gone a-hunting.
Rabbit Osceola 3, level 9.

"Willie!" Kate exclaimed. "Stop the horses!"

The Osceola Mine

When Willie pulled the horses over, Kate showed him the note. For a moment he studied the words.

"Level," Willie said thoughtfully. "Around here, that means only one thing—the level of a mine."

Kate grinned. "That's what I thought. And the rabbit? It must be the treasure!"

Willie nodded. "If it is, those kegs are in shaft number 3, level 9." He, too, looked excited.

"So, we're at the right mine!" Kate exclaimed. "All we have to do is get inside."

"Good thing it's not a C & H mine!" Willie told her. "They've had so many fires it takes an act of the president to get someone down. But with Osceola, I'll get us in."

When Willie started to turn the horses around, Erik asked him to stop. "How do we know this isn't a trap?"

"We don't," Kate answered. She thought back over the different messages. "The note with the rose—that was different paper and different handwriting. This is different paper—trashy paper that looks as if someone picked it up. But the handwriting is the same as for all the rhymes hidden at the mansion."

"It seems too easy," Megan said. "Driving up, finding the note like that."

"Naw!" Anders told her. "Just the luck of the Irish. Right, Kate?"

"What if that man planted the note to make sure we'd follow him? If he wants us out of the way—" Megan stopped as though she couldn't finish the thought.

"And he *does* want us out of the way." Erik looked grim. "He needs to get the treasure out of town as soon as he can. That probably means tonight."

"So is the note a trap?" Kate asked. "Or is it real? That's what we need to know."

"But what if we don't believe the note?" Anders asked. "We don't have any other lead."

In the end they decided to vote on it. Anders and Willie said yes; Megan and Erik said no. That gave Kate the deciding vote.

She had to admit she felt uneasy too. At the same time she didn't know what else to try. They couldn't take a chance on that man getting away.

When Kate voted in favor of trying the mine, Willie started back to the Osceola. This time he saw his uncle outside the shafthouse.

Uncle Tom had the same dark brown eyes as Willie, but also a well-trimmed handlebar mustache. When Willie introduced them, his uncle stretched out a hand to Anders and Erik. To Kate and Megan he offered a warm smile.

"So you have a mystery to solve," he said when Willie explained what they needed. "Or maybe you're trying to get your friends down in the mine?"

Willie grinned. "This time I'm telling the truth. We need to find four nail kegs. We think a man took them down to the ninth level."

"If he did, they'll be easy to find. We aren't working that level anymore, so we wouldn't use nails for track."

But Uncle Tom still looked doubtful. "You're sure about all this, Willie?"

"Yes, sir." Willie went back over the reasons for what they believed.

Finally his uncle said, "Well, I've always wanted to find that treasure myself. Wait half an hour till the day shift leaves, and I'll take you down."

When his uncle hurried off, Willie told them that on Saturday night the mine would be empty. The mining companies gave Sunday off for men to go to church.

While they waited, Willie explained how rock with copper in it came out of the mine in skips—cars that ran on steel rails. A set of tracks led out of the shafthouse to the top of a tall building called the rockhouse. There crushers broke the rock into smaller pieces. The pieces then went to a stamp mill where they were ground into fine powder and the copper taken out.

Willie led them to the boiler house, then the engine house. Through a window Kate saw a huge hoist that looked like a gigantic round drum with grooves for holding heavy cables. The cables brought the skips filled with rock up from the mine.

By now men were coming out of the dry, the building where miners changed their sweaty clothes for dry ones. As Kate and the others waited, they saw Tom go inside.

"Every miner has a coin with a number on it," Willie explained. "Before Uncle Tom goes down in the mine, he needs to leave his number. When he comes back out, he'll pick it up again."

Willie looked at Kate. "I don't think you and Megan should go with us."

"Are you serious?" Kate stared at him.

"A mine can be really dangerous. Sometimes rock falls in. Dynamite goes off—"

"I thought you said the mine would be empty."

"You could fall down a shaft," Willie went on, as though he hadn't heard Kate. "Or into a pit of water. If something happens to the hoist, you'll have to climb the ladders."

"We can manage!" Kate told him, and Megan agreed.

As soon as Willie's uncle returned, he took them to the shafthouse. There he took a hunk of brownish wax, cut pieces, and put them inside what looked like a tiny teakettle. A thick wick came up the spout of the teakettle, or Sunshine lamp as Willie called it.

Uncle Tom slipped the U-shaped handle of the lamp into the front of his hard hat. He filled and lit other lamps for the hard hats he gave each of them, then led them over to a large opening in the ground.

The incline shaft slanted down into the earth. On one side, a set of railroad tracks dropped away. Next to them was a long ladder, attached to the slanted rock walls.

Uncle Tom led them to a man car, a steel and wood car with seats that looked like a stairway. When everyone was seated, Tom pulled a signal rope. The car moved rapidly downward.

At each level, horizontal openings, or drifts, ran off to the right and left. When the car stopped, the ninth level was completely dark. Farther down the shaft, Kate saw the faint glow of lights from a level still being worked.

"Which direction?" Uncle Tom asked as all of them climbed from the man car. "Do you know?"

When Willie shook his head, Tom took them into the drift leading off to the left. Megan put her hand on Kate's shoulder and stayed slightly behind. Walking around a steel tram car filled with rocks, they followed railroad tracks into the darkness. Each Sunshine lamp offered only a faint glow—the light of about three candles.

I'm glad Willie's uncle is with us! Kate thought as the darkness closed in around her.

Once Tom stopped to show them a vein of copper-bearing rock. Megan reached out to feel the wall.

"It's eerie," she whispered to Kate. "Everything echoes so."

Before long, they came to a large opening. Miners had drilled out rock, making a stope. In the large cavelike area pieces of rock still lay scattered around, offering good hiding places. Kate and the boys searched quickly but found nothing.

Farther on, rock had fallen into the drift—the opening where they walked. Tom led them around the rock. At each place where the kegs could be hidden, he helped them look.

Finally they came to the end of the drift. Only a rock wall faced them.

"Well, there's nothing here," Tom said. "Let's try the north side of the shaft."

Turning around, he headed back in the direction from which they came. Anders, Erik, and Willie stayed close behind, asking questions as they walked. Kate and Megan followed the others.

Where the drift passed over the open shaft, there was a wooden floor that reminded Kate of a bridge. On one side the wall went straight up. On the other side a railing protected them from falling into the shaft. As Kate and Megan stepped onto the wood, their footsteps echoed. Kate held her breath, just thinking about the empty space below them.

Halfway across the shaft there was a hole for dumping rock from a tram car into the skip that took it to the surface. Kate stepped around the hole, leading Megan. Just beyond was a smaller hole for stepping onto the ladder that led upward.

Beyond the shaft, they searched again, following the drift through the cavelike stopes. Finally Tom stopped. "This rock looks loose. I don't want to take you any farther. I think someone was trying to fool you."

"If he did, he drove away with the kegs," Kate muttered to Megan. "Probably while the shift was changing."

Turning around, Tom again started back to the shaft. The boys followed. Not wanting to give up the search, Kate walked more slowly. As she and Megan passed beneath a low overhang, a few pebbles trickled to the ground.

Kate tugged Megan's arm, yanked her out of the way. The small rocks fell off to the side, three or four feet from the girls.

Ahead of them, Tom whirled around. Just then another dribble of rock slid down the wall. As Tom's lamp focused on the wall, the dribble became a small stream.

"Look out!" he called, his voice urgent. "Run!"

In front of Kate, a larger rock tumbled to the ground. In the next instant Kate turned back, pulled Megan with her. Heading away from the others, they ran for their lives.

"Hurry!" Tom shouted from somewhere behind them.

As bigger rocks tumbled down, Megan stumbled on a track. Kate held her up, and they hurried on, trying to get beyond the falling rock.

"Kate!" Erik's frantic voice seemed far away. "Kate!"

Suddenly a noise like thunder exploded behind Kate. As she fell to the ground, Megan landed beside her.

The last thing Kate heard was Erik's voice calling her. Then a wall of rock settled between them.

19

Trapped!

A stone hit Kate's hard hat, jarring her head. The thunder seemed to last forever. The stillness that followed was even more awful.

"Megan?" Kate called out. A knot twisted her insides. "Are you all right?"

"I'm fine," Megan answered from close beside Kate. "Are you?"

Kate started to say yes, then realized she could barely see. Somehow her light had gone out.

"I think so," Kate said slowly. Yet she could not push away her panic. "What happened to my light?"

Reaching up, Kate felt the front of her hard hat. Her Sunshine lamp was gone!

"That rock! It must have knocked off my lamp!"

One moment Kate felt the awfulness of it. The next instant she felt grateful that the hat protected her head. But then Kate realized what had really happened.

She jumped to her feet. "Erik!" she called. "Erik!"

From the darkness no one answered.

"Erik!" Kate shouted again. His was the last voice she heard. Did that mean he was closest to the falling rock?

Tears blurred Kate's vision. What could be worse than having something happen to Erik?

In that instant Kate remembered her brother. "Anders!" she called. "Anders!"

Again, only silence greeted her ears. Kate's chest tightened. Could Anders be buried beneath the cave-in? In that moment all of Kate's disagreements with Anders fell away. In spite of his teasing, he was a brother she loved.

Standing near Kate, Megan shouted for Willie, then his uncle. The walls echoed back, seeming to mock them.

In the cool dampness of the mine Kate shivered. She tried to tell herself that things would be all right. But she could not stop trembling.

"I'm so scared!" she wailed. "Oh, God, please help us!"

"Willie! Tom!" Megan called again and again until her voice turned hoarse.

"When we ran this way, they must have gone the other direction," Kate said finally. "And the rock settled between us."

"Maybe they ran really fast." Megan answered quickly, as if not wanting to think about any other possibility.

In the dim light the darkness closed in around Kate. For a frantic moment she wondered if she could smother.

"Here, take my lamp, Megan said, as though guessing how Kate felt. "I don't need it."

As Kate reached out, Megan gave her a hug. For the first time since the ceiling caved in, Kate felt as though she could think. Carefully she slipped Megan's lamp into her own hard hat.

The great heap of rock lay dangerously close to where the girls had landed on the ground. At first Kate searched quickly, looking for any sign of Tom or the boys. Pushed on by panic, Kate moved her head from side to side, trying to see everything at once.

Then she forced herself to stand still. Taking one section at a time, she directed the beam of light onto the rocks. As the light passed from one wall of the drift to the other, Kate looked for any small piece of clothing, any sign of her lamp. More than once, she moved forward to check a shadow.

Standing back again, Kate tipped her head up and down. As the beam of light reached the ceiling, her panic returned. Huge boulders filled the entire opening. Even if she and Megan were strong enough to move the rocks, it would take days to make a small hole.

Kate groaned. She wanted to rush toward the rocks, to pound them with her fists. "I'm the one who decided we'd come down here! It's all my fault!"

In one flash Kate remembered her talk with Willie. With all her heart Kate had meant every word she said. Yet now, none of those comforting words about Megan's accident seemed big enough. Not if someone lay beneath those rocks.

"Kate!" Megan called from where she stood. "What did you find?"

Filled with despair, Kate returned to her cousin. Kate could barely speak. "I can't tell if anyone's under those rocks!"

In the dim light, Megan reached out. Her hand felt cold and clammy, and Kate knew it was more than the coolness of the mine. Though she tried to seem calm, Megan was just as afraid.

"It was a trap, wasn't it?" Kate's anger spilled out. "You were right. It was a trap!"

"I think so," Megan answered.

"That crook—that Curly! Fooling us into coming down in the mine!" Kate wanted to scream at him. "I bet he's moving the treasure tonight and wanted to make sure we were somewhere else."

Kate felt as if the ceiling were falling again. "That stupid treasure! It's not worth having people get killed!"

Great sobs rose in her throat. "We're cut off! The whole opening is closed!"

"We need to pray," Megan answered quietly.

Kate shuddered. She had all she could do not to panic. Trying to push the darkness away, she drew a deep breath.

When Kate could speak, they prayed together. Megan asked that all of them could get out safely, without anything more happening.

"And, God, help us know what to do," Kate added.

When they finished, Kate's stomach was still tied in knots, her fear still there. At the same time she felt peaceful. It surprised her.

In that moment there was something she knew. They hadn't come down here just looking for treasure. All of them had wanted something more. For Megan to be safe from that man named Curly. For good to win over evil.

Once more, Kate looked back toward the great heap of fallen rock. Then she turned, facing the other direction.

"We have to keep going," she told Megan.

"Maybe there's another shaft in that direction," Megan said.

"But how do we know?" Kate asked.

"When we were still outside—when Willie showed us around, did you see a shafthouse off that way?"

Kate had to think about it. Yes, there were other shafthouses in the area. But had any of them been in the direction they needed to go?

"I think so," Kate finally answered, wishing she could be more sure.

In the dim light Megan looked troubled. "Even if there's a shaft-house, we don't know if we're on a level that connects with it. And there's—"

"There's what?" Kate asked.

Megan hesitated, as if not wanting to tell her. "Sometimes mines have to seal off a shaft—close the entrance. C & H did that to stop fires in their mines."

"So if we do get to the top—" Kate didn't want to finish the thought.

"It might not be open," Megan said.

In that moment Kate remembered their only remaining lamp. She reached up and felt the Sunshine lamp Megan had given her. "How long will this last? When does it run out of fuel?"

Megan shrugged. "Willie says the men carry extra wax down with them."

"So our light won't last a whole shift," Kate said. "A shift is ten hours. The lamp might go out in half that time!"

She grabbed Megan's hand. "Let's get going!"

Ahead of them, the drift soon widened into the large hollowed-out area of a stope. As Kate tipped back her head, her light shone upward for several hundred feet.

Then she looked down. The huge cavern dropped away into the blackness of the workings below. Kate caught her breath. One wrong step and they would fall to certain death.

Clenching Megan's hand, Kate backed away from the edge of the hole. With all the strength she had, Kate forced herself to continue walking. Every step felt as if it would be her last.

As they passed beyond the hole, Kate drew a sigh of relief. But then a few steps farther on, she saw something swoop toward her. When she ducked, Megan stumbled.

"What's wrong?" she asked.

Moments later Kate's light caught wings heading straight toward them. Her heart thudding, Kate pulled Megan down.

"Bats!" Kate cried, filled with the horror of it. "There are bats in here!"

Megan shuddered. "What if they fly into our faces?"

Huddling there, Kate covered her head, wishing she could crawl under a blanket. Then she remembered the lamp, their need for light. Much as she wanted to hide, they had to go on.

For what seemed an eternity Kate led Megan past huge hollowed-out areas with only a few pillars for support. Then the drift narrowed with little room on either side of the rails.

Kate's grip tightened. Again Megan asked what was wrong.

"We're running out of places to go." Kate's free hand tightened into a nervous fist.

Soon the walls again opened into a larger area. Feeling relieved, Kate picked up her pace. With all her heart she wanted to escape the darkness. One side of the rock floor sloped downward. Anxious to find another shaft, Kate moved quickly in spite of the slanting floor.

Megan tugged her hand. "Wait!" she said. "I hear dripping!"

Kate jerked to a stop. Standing still, she listened. Megan was right. Kate heard it now. Water dripping on water.

Afraid to move, Kate turned only her head. To her left, across an open area, the beam of light shone on straight up and down walls. The walls ended in a deep pit.

As Kate looked down, her heart thudded. Close by, only two feet away from where she stood, was the nearest side of the pit. Here the rock ended, level with the path. Kate's lamp caught the reflection of water.

Carefully she edged back. In a few more steps she would have fallen into the water, taking Megan with her. The sheer walls offered no hope of getting out.

Just then Kate's lamp flickered. Desperately she stared ahead, taking one final look. The next instant the light flickered out.

New Danger

Kate clung to Megan's hand, feeling that if she lost it, she'd never find Megan again.

"Our light," Kate said weakly. She remembered Willie's uncle filling the lamps. With all her heart Kate wished she had some of that wax now. "We lost our light."

From the darkness, Kate heard a gasp. But when Megan spoke, she only said, "What was the last thing you saw?"

When Kate described it for her, Megan answered, "Let me go first."

Kate's heart thudded. Only a few days before, she had talked to the others about her cousin's blindness. "Megan's going to do everything we do!" Kate had said.

Now she faced perhaps the biggest danger of her life. *I've always led everyone else*, Kate thought. *Should I let someone who's blind lead me?* Her knees felt weak just thinking about it.

Megan tugged her hand. "Move back," she said, forcing Kate's decision.

When they changed places, Megan stood still for a moment, as if listening. "The water was to your left?" she asked, but it was not really a question.

Once again they started out, this time with Megan in the lead. In the darkness Kate heard Megan shuffle her feet, as though feeling around. Inch by inch they crept forward with Megan leading Kate.

On the narrow path Kate's left foot was lower than the right. Near at hand, the water dripped. Kate tried not to think about the pit only a few feet away.

Her hand clenching Kate's, Megan shuffled on. As though she could see her cousin, Kate imagined Megan's free hand reaching out in the darkness.

Before long, Kate's muscles ached with tension. After what seemed forever, the rock floor evened out.

"The water's behind," Megan said.

Kate listened. When had the dripping stopped? All she could think about was the hideous darkness.

A bit farther on, Kate felt a wall on her right. When the wall disappeared, Megan stopped.

"Talk, Kate," she said. "The echo helps me."

Kate talked, saying anything that came into her head. Now and then Megan stopped, seeming to listen. Once again, Kate felt a wall, then an openness.

Moments later the floor changed from rock to hollow-sounding wood. "We found a shaft!" Megan exclaimed.

Kate's stomach tightened as she remembered the long drop beneath the wooden floor that covered the shaft like a bridge.

Judging by the sound on the wood, Megan was shuffling her feet. "Stand still," she said as she dropped Kate's hand.

"There are holes in the floor!" Kate said quickly. As though she were still seeing the first shaft, she described the large hole for dumping rock and the barricade around it. Beyond that was the smaller, unprotected hole for the ladder.

Both girls dropped to their knees. Staying close, they crawled across the wooden floor over the shaft.

Together they found the hole for dropping rock into a skip. Moving beyond, they continued to search.

"Kate?" Megan asked suddenly. "You have to reach across the hole for the ladder?"

In the darkness Kate felt Megan lean forward, reaching out.

"If you miss, you'll fall," Kate warned.

But Megan was creeping forward on her knees. Suddenly she cried out, "I've got it! I found the ladder!"

Taking Kate's hand, Megan pulled her close to the hole in the floor. Kate felt paralyzed by her fear of what she could not see. But Megan set her own hand down on a rung of the ladder. The wood was slippery with dampness.

"It's wet," Megan said. "We've got to be careful."

"Careful!" Nervously Kate giggled.

As Megan stepped onto the ladder, Kate felt her cousin's movement in the darkness. Kate had no choice but to follow. *Nine levels?* she asked herself. *That's nine hundred feet!* She didn't want to think what it would mean if she fell.

Partway up, Kate's foot slipped. Soon after, she heard Megan cry out in the darkness.

More than once they stopped to rest and catch their breath. Each time they did, Kate had to push away her fears about what had happened to the others.

It seemed hours before they climbed out into a shafthouse. The large room was dark with the deeper shadows of machinery. Kate stumbled around, trying to find a light switch without falling back into the shaft.

She was still searching when a door opened. As light flooded the building, Kate saw Erik running toward her. Directly in front of her he stopped, as though unable to believe she was there.

"Oh, Kate!" Erik's face was gray-white. "You sure know how to worry a fellow!"

"You're alive?" Kate asked, barely able to speak. "You're really alive?"

Then Anders was there. "Please, Kate, don't ever do *that* again!"

Kate stared up at him. "You're not hurt?" She felt weak with relief.

"We're all right," Erik assured her. "Are you and Megan?"

Kate nodded, but in that instant all of her fears broke loose. She began to tremble. Then her body shook with sobs, and she could not stop weeping.

When at last Kate drew a long, shuddering breath, she felt embarrassed. Then her gaze met Erik's. He was crying too.

Kate wanted to tell him how she felt when she thought that he and Anders lay beneath the rocks. Yet she couldn't get out the words.

Awkwardly Anders patted Kate's shoulder, yanked her braid. "Good to see you, sis." His voice broke, as if he, too, were pushing aside tears.

Only then did Kate realize that Megan was standing behind her.

"Willie?" Megan asked. "Did he get hurt?"

"He's coming," Anders told her.

Before long, Willie hurried into the shafthouse. When he saw Megan, his eyes lit up with relief.

"Megan led me out," Kate said. She wanted everyone to know. "There was a deep hole with straight up and down sides. It was full of water, and I almost walked into it. Then we didn't have a light, but Megan got us out." Kate squeezed her cousin's hand, then hugged her.

But Megan brushed it aside as if she had only done what she needed to do. "Your Uncle Tom?" she asked Willie.

"He was trying to help us and got the worst of the rock," Willie said.

At first the boys thought Tom had been buried. Then they found him knocked unconscious, lying on the floor and wedged between two rocks. His leg lay at a strange angle.

Willie had hurried back to the shaft. He knew the signals and called the man working the hoist to ask for help. The men who came down worked with the boys to move the rocks. One of the men splinted Tom's leg. They managed to carry him out without more injury.

"He's on the way to the hospital," Willie said.

For the first time Kate noticed the miners standing nearby.

When they went outside, day had turned to night. As they started back to the shafthouse where they entered the mine, Willie told them more.

"They took Uncle Tom away on a stretcher, and he looked real bad. But he said, 'I'll be all right. You be careful.' "

"What did he mean?" Kate asked.

"When we tried to move the rocks, I was really upset. As soon as Uncle Tom came to, he asked questions. He told us where to search for you and Megan. Then he said, 'Just make sure your side wins.' "

Willie took Megan's hand. "Come on, Meg," he said. "We're going to make sure you win."

When they came to a road, Willie started to run, and Megan followed, lightly holding his arm. Side by side, they kept the same pace. Megan ran as though she had wings, like a bird let out of a cage.

Suddenly Kate remembered. "I like to run," Megan had said. "I like feeling the wind in my hair." As they reached the first shafthouse, Kate saw the joy in her cousin's face.

All of them tumbled into the buggy, and Willie flicked the reins.

"We don't have much time," Kate said. Climbing up that endless ladder, she had thought about it. "Curly must have driven to this mine, knowing we'd follow. To make sure we'd go down, he left that piece of paper. He's probably trying to get away right this minute!"

"But where did he go from there?" Anders asked. "Where are the kegs? That's what we have to know!"

With no other leads, they decided to go back to the mansion. Kate wanted to see if they would find a new message.

"Whatever we do, we've got to be quiet," she warned. "Someone knows every move we make."

When they reached the mansion, Willie directed the horses to the stable. Kate slipped down and hurried around the mansion. Without making a sound, she pulled out the loose brick, then a message. Holding it toward the streetlight, she read the words:

> Mary, Mary, quite contrary,
> How does your treasure grow?
> With silver bells and cockle shells,
> And four kegs all in a row.
>
> Hickory, dickory, dock,
> The mouse ran up the clock.
> The clock struck one.

Quickly Kate memorized the rhymes, slipped the note back, and replaced the brick.

"One o'clock!" she told the others. They had gone inside the stable and closed the door. "At one o'clock the treasure goes out! We haven't got much time!"

"But *where* does it go out?" Anders asked. "On a train, do you think?"

"It must be in the first rhyme." Kate repeated that rhyme and they all agreed.

"What's a cockle shell?" Kate asked. "It makes me think of water. And so does the word *dock*."

Suddenly she laughed. "Maybe that's it! We're close to Lake Superior. How could someone load kegs onto a ship?"

"Torch Lake!" Megan exclaimed.

"The ore boats!" Willie said at the same moment.

"What do you mean?" Kate asked.

Willie lit a lantern, picked up a stick, and drew in the soft ground inside the stable. "Here's the Keweenaw Peninsula," he said. "See how Lake Superior surrounds it? That's how early settlers came ashore— boats landed. We had the first mineral rush in the U.S.A."

"Before the California gold rush!" Megan looked excited now.

"But Lake Superior is dangerous. Storms come up really fast," Willie said. "So men built Portage Canal. In bad weather, ships get off Lake Superior and hide in here."

Willie drew a line from Lake Superior to what he called the Lily Pond. "A ship can go all the way through the Portage Canal to the other side of the Keweenaw Peninsula. Or it can pass out of Portage Lake through a channel into Torch Lake."

Willie drew again. "Here's Torch Lake. Along the shore there's a bunch of stamp mills and the village of Lake Linden. Here's the smelter at Hubbell."

"And ships come into Torch Lake?" Kate asked.

"Bringing coal and taking out copper," Willie told her.

"What about at night?" Erik asked. "The rhyme says one o'clock. Can ships go through the channel at night?"

"Sure thing!" Willie answered. "There are seven little lighthouses along the way."

Kate jumped up. "That's it!"

"The lighthouses?" Megan sounded puzzled.

"No!" Kate exclaimed. "Remember the book about the smugglers of Cornwall? Someone read the book *we* read! That's why it was out on the table in Mr. Mitchell's library. The smugglers hid their kegs in the water—all in a row!"

Erik laughed. "And the smugglers took their kegs on a wagon, right through town. What could be better hidden than something really obvious?"

"And then the smugglers took the kegs out of the water when it was safe!" Anders exclaimed. "Let's go!"

Each of the boys grabbed a lantern. Quietly they all slipped out and climbed into the buggy.

As they passed from the driveway into the street, Kate turned around. The next time she saw the mansion, the mystery might be solved. The Mitchells would no longer be troubled, and Megan would be safe!

The mansion was dark, but the streetlight shone on one of the windows. Behind the glass, the curtain dropped back in place.

Surprise for Kate

The road took them past the mansions of Laurium, but Kate barely noticed. She kept thinking about what she had seen.

I imagined it, she told herself. *The house is empty. It was just a trick of the light.*

Yet Kate couldn't push away her uneasiness. Was someone there, after all? Someone who knew they had driven in, then out again? *Maybe it really was Tisha at the theater! When Willie let her off at the depot, she could have slipped away.*

Before long, the buggy brought them to the top of a steep hill. Nearby, a high trestle supported railroad tracks from the top of the hill to the valley below. In the moonlight Kate saw a number of tall smokestacks off in the distance.

As they entered the village of Lake Linden, Kate again noticed the trestle. Tracks led directly to the top of a tall building for cars to drop rock into the stamp mill.

Willie turned right onto a street running parallel to Torch Lake. More mills—the ones Kate had seen from above—stood between the street and the water.

Close to a building, a large ore ship waited. At another dock a hoist had unloaded a great mound of coal. Seeing all the places to hide something, Kate wondered how they could possibly find the kegs filled with silver.

Willie turned back toward Kate. "Where do I go?"

Kate didn't know. "Would Curly try to get those kegs on an ore ship?"

Willie shrugged. "People would ask questions."

"How about a smaller boat?" Kate asked. "Would that work?"

They looked for a place where a man could drive down to Torch Lake without people being curious. They found two possible places with a path wide enough for a wagon. Anders and Megan dropped down from the buggy at the first, and Willie left Kate and Erik at the second.

Quickly Erik lit their lantern. A large building lay on one side of the dirt path. On the other side, the path gave way to weeds and bushes.

Watching for anything unusual, Erik and Kate followed the path toward Torch Lake. Halfway to the water, Erik stopped for a closer look.

"That's it!" he whispered. He held the light next to a wagon track. "See the slash mark across the right rear wheel? It's the same mark we saw before!"

The dirt was soft, and they followed the wagon track right up to the water.

"Well," Kate said. "Guess we go swimming."

She and Erik pulled off their shoes and hid them in tall weeds. Erik left the lantern on shore. Walking about ten feet apart, they waded into the water.

"Be careful, Kate," Erik whispered. "You don't know how deep it is."

"I can swim," she said lightly. Everything seemed easy, now that Erik was all right.

In the moonlight the water looked cold and black, but Kate waded on. With every step she swung her feet around, hoping to hit a keg under water. Erik stayed even with her, searching the same way.

The water remained shallow for some distance before a wave caught the bottom of Kate's dress. Gradually the water reached her waist. Still she found nothing.

Finally Kate stopped, turned around, and looked back toward shore. The tall smokestacks rose above everything else—a dark outline against the night sky. If the kegs were here, there had to be a way to mark where they were hidden.

Then Kate saw it. Near the lighted lantern there was a tall post along the shore. The water had reached Kate's chest now, but she lined herself up with the post. A moment later her foot felt something hard!

Diving beneath the surface, Kate found a chain, then a keg. When she surfaced again, she lifted her arm in victory.

Erik grinned, then looked toward shore, as though he, too, marked the spot in his mind. Then he and Kate waded back.

They had barely stepped out of the water when Kate heard someone on the road. Snatching up the lantern, Erik blew it out, then led Kate through the weeds. When they reached tall bushes, they stepped behind them.

Looking back between the leaves, Kate saw the shapes of two men, both dressed in business suits. Each wore a hat, but darkness hid their faces. One was slightly smaller than the other.

Together they pulled a boat out of the weeds, tipped it over, and set oars inside. As the smaller man climbed in, the other spoke softly.

Kate recognized the voice. "It's Curly!"

A moment later, Curly pushed the boat into the water. Hopping in, he sat down and began to row.

"They'll get the treasure and get away," Kate whispered. "If they reach Portage Canal, we'll never find them again."

"Let's pretend we've been swimming," Erik said softly. "It's dark enough so they can't see who we are."

Boldly they walked out of the bushes. Erik rescued their shoes from the weeds. Sitting down on the shore, they pulled them on.

Erik smiled at Kate, spoke in a voice that would carry. "You're pretty, even when you're wet."

Kate caught her breath, taken off guard. Did he mean it? Or was he saying that for the people in the boat?

Erik didn't give her time to think about it. Catching Kate's hand, he helped her up, then started walking. As though they were out for a midnight stroll, he walked slowly, and Kate followed.

Once he leaned close, whispered softly. "Just do what I do," he said.

As they reached the corner of the nearby building, Erik turned toward it. Once he glanced toward the lake, but always he walked as if he had all the time in the world. When they slipped behind the building, he started running.

"Let's get the others!" He pulled Kate along.

Just when Kate thought she could run no farther, she saw a movement in the shadows next to another building. It was Anders, Megan, and Willie.

"Go for the watchman," Erik told Willie. "Bring him to the place where you left us!"

As Willie took off at a run, Erik explained to Anders and Megan. "There are two people in a boat. Let's make sure they don't get away."

Staying on the short grass at the edge of the road, the four hurried back to where the kegs were hidden. Without making a sound, they dropped down next to the building, deep within its shadow. From there Kate could see gentle waves rocking the boats. The two dark figures sat without moving.

"What's happening?" Megan whispered.

Afraid that her voice would carry, Kate put her mouth against Megan's ear. "Curly and another man are in a boat. I think they're making sure that we're gone."

For at least twenty minutes more the men waited. Kate and the others waited too. At last Curly lifted a long pole. Dipping it down in the water, he felt around.

After a few tries, he moved the boat so it was more in line with the post Kate had noticed. This time the pole caught a chain.

The second man reached down, tugged at the chain. A keg appeared, and Curly pulled it closer. When he tried to lift the keg, it splashed back in the water.

"Stupid! Watch what you're doing!" a low voice hissed. Across the water the words came clearly.

"What's Tisha doing here?" Megan spoke into Kate's ear.

"Tisha?" Kate whispered back. The question caught Kate by surprise. "Why do you ask?"

"That's her voice. What's she doing here?"

"We thought she was a man."

Megan shook her head. "It's Tisha. Be careful. She's got an awful kick."

In the darkness Kate smothered a giggle. After all that had happened, she felt weak with laughter. Elegant Tisha having an awful kick? It seemed too strange to believe.

Besides, it was a man with Curly in the boat. Kate was sure of it.

"You don't believe me, do you?" Megan whispered. "It's true. I saw her kick a cat once."

No doubt the cat had hissed and howled, and Megan knew exactly what happened. But the idea of Tisha kicking someone still struck Kate funny.

Next to Kate, Anders moved restlessly. "If they get the silver, they'll row away," he whispered.

Once again Curly pulled in the keg. On his second try, he managed to get it into the rowboat.

Erik shifted his position. "Where's Willie?" he asked. "The rest of you stay here. If I can't find a watchman, I'll try the police."

A moment later, Erik disappeared into the night.

As Kate watched, Curly pulled in the second keg, then the third and the fourth. He was on his knees, leaning over the side, when the smaller man moved close and gave a quick kick. In the next instant Kate heard a loud splash.

A dark head appeared in the water. "Help!" Curly cried. "I can't swim!" Frantically he waved his arms.

The man in the boat leaped toward the oars. For an instant Kate thought he would offer one to Curly. Instead, the man sat down and rowed away.

"Help!" Curly cried again. "Help!"

Frantically Kate glanced around for a branch or stick. Instead, she found a long pole. She and Anders ran into the lake, wading as fast as they could in the shallow water.

Ahead of them, Curly disappeared. A moment later, he surfaced just beyond the drop-off.

Anders held out the pole. Curly's arms thrashed, but he managed to reach it.

Kate and Anders pulled him toward shore. As they reached the beach, Willie and Erik ran up. With them were four men.

As though Curly didn't see them, he dropped to the ground, too weak to stand.

"Tisha?" he asked. Seeming confused, he looked out over the water.

"She got away," Kate said.

Curly clenched his fists. "She betrayed me."

His voice rose in anger. "Had me do her dirty work! Then she steals the loot."

"Do you know where she's going?" Kate asked.

"Sure thing. I'll go after her. I'll teach her a lesson." Curly struggled up, but sank back, exhausted.

"Where's she's going?" Kate asked quickly.

Curly hesitated. For the first time he noticed the men standing nearby.

"It'll go easier for you if you tell us," a policeman promised.

And so, Curly told them how he met Tisha soon after each of them had heard the story about the lost treasure. Always Tisha had been the boss, while he carried out her orders. They had planned to row out through the canal to a place on the shores of Portage Lake. From there they would carry the silver nuggets away.

"Fool that I am!" Curly exclaimed. "I was an honest man till I met her!"

* * * * *

On Sunday afternoon the Mitchells returned home. Soon after they arrived, Megan slipped over to the mansion. When she returned with Willie, Megan told Kate and Anders and Erik that Mr. Mitchell would like to see them.

Mr. Mitchell wanted to know every detail of what had happened. Finally he said, "Now, what shall we do with the silver nuggets?" He looked from one to the other.

It was Erik who answered. "They're yours, sir. Payment on that loan your father gave."

But Mr. Mitchell shook his head. "That silver has caused so much trouble, let's put it to some good use."

He thought for a moment, then said, "I'd like to help each of you get some training. Yet I'm afraid to give you all the money you need. If I do, you might not appreciate your schooling."

Mr. Mitchell looked from one to another. "I'll think of a way where you need to work for what you want, but I'll still give you some help. What do you want to be when you grow up?"

"A great organist," Kate said quickly. "And I want to play the piano and teach music."

"You do?" Megan asked in surprise. "Maybe that's what I could be—a music teacher!"

"And you, Anders?" Mr. Mitchell asked.

"I want to stay on the farm, sir. I want to learn whatever I need to be the best farmer I can."

"Erik?"

"I believe I know, but I want to think about it more before I say. I'll need to go to school for a long time."

He never says, Kate thought. *I wonder what he's planning to be?* Always she wanted to know.

"Willie, what about you?" Mr. Mitchell asked. "Casey tells me you have a quick mind."

"Is there something—" Willie glanced toward Megan. "Is there something where I can help people who are blind? Help them do all the things that Megan does?"

Mr. Mitchell nodded, a strange expression on his face. Had he also noticed how Willie treated Megan only a week before? As Megan turned toward Willie, all their fights seemed forgotten.

Mr. Mitchell stretched out his hand, thanked each of them in turn. But he stopped in front of Kate.

"Megan tells me you're the one who figured out where Curly put the kegs of silver. And you and Anders helped Curly so he didn't drown. I want to give you something extra right now—the money to buy your own horse."

"A horse?" Kate blurted out. "How did you know I want a horse?"

"Megan told me. You can have your father and Anders help you pick it out."

Kate couldn't believe it. "My own horse!" If Mr. Mitchell hadn't been standing in front of her, she would have leaped up and down.

The next afternoon it was time for Kate and the boys to leave for home. Saying goodbye was even more difficult than Kate had expected. She hugged Cousin Breda, thanking her for all it had meant to be with them.

"You'll come and visit us?" Kate asked more than once. Though she had known Megan's family only a week, they already filled her heart.

Cousin Casey led Kate around the apartment in a final jig. He grinned and teased the whole way, but when Kate told him goodbye, tears welled up in his blue eyes.

"Sure and we'll see you again," he promised. "Tell your mother she raised a good daughter."

His quick gaze took in Anders. "And a good son."

Then Casey tipped his head toward Erik and winked at Kate. "It's one grand friend you and Anders have. Am I going to see him too?"

Kate shrugged, trying to pretend it wasn't important. Yet she felt the hot flush of embarrassment creep into her cheeks. She hoped Erik wouldn't notice.

"Maybe I'll come to your wedding someday," Casey said.

Kate stole a glance at Erik. He didn't even seem embarrassed. Instead, Erik grinned at Casey.

"Well!" Kate said. "If that's going to happen, whoever I marry will have to get Papa's approval!"

Willie drove all of them to the Mineral Range Depot. There Kate discovered that it was hardest of all to say goodbye to Megan. In one short week they had become close friends.

Soon it was time to climb aboard the train. Kate gave Megan a final hug, then quickly turned away. But Megan's voice followed her.

"I'll never forget our times together!" Megan said. "I'll never forget what you mean to me!"

"We'll ride the bicycle together!" Willie called.

Inside the railroad car, Kate found a seat on the side toward the depot. Holding back her tears, she leaned out the window and waved. Though Megan couldn't see, she would know.

"Goodbye, Megan!" Kate called as the train wheels started to turn. "Goodbye!"

Her cousin turned toward the sound of Kate's voice and waved with all her might. As the train chugged away, Megan said something to Willie. Then her face grew smaller and smaller.

At last Kate leaned back against the seat. With a lump in her throat, she sat quietly for a long time, unable to speak. *I'm going to see her again*, Kate promised herself. *Megan really will come to Windy Hill Farm!*

Finally Kate turned to her brother Anders and to Erik, their special friend. "Just think of all the fun we can have when I get a horse!"

Acknowledgments

When I was a child, I met a very special man named John Erickson. Though John was blind, he and his family lived a full and active life.

As John's children and I played hide-and-seek with a button, one of the girls hid the button behind her father's dark glasses. Those glasses seemed a normal part of living. Somehow I never forgot.

Years later, when my husband and I visited a camp in Wisconsin, an eleven-year-old girl named AnnaLisa Anderson stood up to sing. I admired her ability at such a young age, then realized that she was blind. Again, it was something I never forgot.

By now, AnnaLisa has graduated from Northwestern College in St. Paul with a major in music. She teaches voice, gives concerts, and works on the Minnesota Relay Service to pass on messages for people with hearing disabilities.

Not all blind people can sing, just as not all sighted people are gifted in music. Megan's story is not exactly the same as AnnaLisa's. Yet AnnaLisa, John, and a woman named Janis Atkins of Janesville, Wisconsin, have given me a love for courage. Each of them has overcome obstacles in order to become a very special person.

As you read this book, you may have wondered, *Why didn't Megan have a guide dog? Or why didn't she use a white cane?*

In these years when people with visual disabilities have a variety of devices to help them, it's hard to realize how different things once were. Now a person with a seeing disability may take classes in the use of a cane. However, in Megan's time a blind child would not have used a cane.

The biggest single breakthrough toward the independence of blind people came with the training of guide dogs. In 1928, a German Shepherd named Buddy became the first guide dog in the United States. John Erickson had a German Shepherd named Chief. AnnaLisa has a chocolate Lab named Megan. (My story character, Megan, was named before I met AnnaLisa's guide dog.) Janis has a black Lab named Emerald.

In Chapter 7 Megan tells Kate that she wants to see her old home at Central Mine. Blind people tend to use words like *see* and *look* because they're part of the vocabulary of the world in which they live.

As AnnaLisa told me, "I *see* things, even though I see them with my hands instead of my eyes."

Though AnnaLisa and Janis write with a slate and stylus, both of them also use a regular computer with a special printer that produces braille. Holly Jensen, a new friend of mine, explained how she uses another breakthrough, a screen reader, to get access to the internet, read, and write using her computer. Her e-mails are beautifully written.

AnnaLisa, Janis, and John have made my life rich. I am deeply grateful to Janis and AnnaLisa and to AnnaLisa's parents, George and Blanche Anderson, for helping me write Megan's story. Thanks to Dr. Bruce E. Benedict for his professional wisdom about Megan's injury.

My gratitude to the Wisconsin School for the Visually Handicapped in Janesville; Mary Archer of the Minnesota State Services for the Blind; Myrna Wright, director of the Minnesota Library for the Blind and Physically Handicapped in Faribault; and Corrine Kirchner, American Foundation for the Blind in New York City.

Kenneth Stuckey, Research Librarian at the Samuel P. Hayes Library, Perkins School for the Blind in Watertown, Massachusetts, gave valuable suggestions and time, provided excellent material, and read the manuscript. Jan Seymour-Ford, Research Librarian at the same school and library, helped me with this edition and additional details about resources for the blind. See *www.perkins.org/researchlibrary* for their online catalog.

While researching for this book, I also discovered another group of people with courage. The copper miners of the Keweenaw Peninsula often faced great dangers in order to earn a living and build a life.

As I learned about their story, Charles Stetter, Laurium historian and former principal of the Calumet High School, generously shared his own writings with me, gave of his time and knowledge, introduced me to a number of other resource people, and read portions of the manuscript. Charles also played an important part in the annual Central Mine reunions, which have been held every year since 1907.

I am also indebted to John Wilson, head patternmaker for the C & H Mine; Jack Foster, C & H security chief and retired Cousin Jack; and Bob Faller, smelter at Hubbell. All provided valuable firsthand information. Former Laurium resident and geologist James Brooks gave me a day-long tour of various mining sites in the Calumet area, answered countless questions, and gave valuable help with the manuscript.

Thanks, also, to these Michigan people: In Calumet, Mary Jane Goraczniak; Stuart Baird, manager, Coppertown USA Mining Museum;

Tony Bausano, manager of the Copper World Bookstore; Vera Stellberg and Robert Thompson, tour guides at the Calumet Theatre; Kay Masters and all who helped me in the archives at the J. Robert Van Pelt Library, Michigan Technological University, Houghton; Julie Blair, archival associate at the MTU Archives & Copper Country Historical Collections, and instructor, Department of Social Sciences, for her help with the Sunshine lamps on the cover. http://www.lib.mtu. edu/mtuarchives/.

I'm also grateful to Maurice Erickson and Jim Hoefler of the Grantsburg, Wisconsin area, and to Sandy Fulton for searching out Megan's song. Thanks to the staff at Pendarvis, the Wisconsin State Historical Society site at Mineral Point; Tim Shandel of the Lake Superior Museum of Transportation, Duluth. Thanks also to David Chancellor, Jim Walfrid, and Kevin Johnson for contributing important ideas used in this novel.

For those of you who wondered, *Minesota* is the correct spelling of that mine. It seems that when the mine was formed, a weary clerk working by candlelight misspelled the name. It was recorded that way by the State of Michigan.

If you visit the Calumet area, you'll find some things have changed. The steeple of the former Red Jacket Opera House has been shortened to avoid lightning strikes. St. Joseph's Catholic Church is now named St. Paul the Apostle.

In Chapter 8 Willie claims that Upper Michigan is the only source of pure copper in the world. This was a common misbelief in 1907, as well as today. Native copper occurs in other areas, such as Pennsylvania, New Jersey, Virginia, Arizona, Mexico, Bolivia, and Cornwall, to name a few. However, it *is* true that Michigan is the only place in the world where the principal ore was native copper.

Through their books, a number of authors have helped me, including Angus Murdoch, *Boom Copper*; John Vivian, *Tales of the Cornish Smugglers*; Paul T. Steele, *Tamarack Town*; Tauno Kilpela, *The Hard Rock Mining Era in the Copper Country*; Clarence J. Monette for his Local History Series; and Ruth R. Hayden, *Erma at Perkins*.

As always, thanks to my agent, Lee Hough, Alive Communications, for his help. For the first edition thank you to the entire Bethany team and my editors, Doris Holmlund, Ron Klug, Lance Wubbels, and Barbara Lilland.

For this edition my gratitude to Joyce Bohn, Glynn Simmons, and all the people at Mott Media. Thanks, Tim Holden, for the awesome cover art!

Finally, thanks to you, Roy, my faithful, supportive husband. Together we explored the Keweenaw Peninsula and camped at beautiful McLain State Park. While there, we watched sunsets and northern lights over Lake Superior and talked about this story. Wasn't it fun?

LaVergne, TN USA
16 March 2010
176169LV00001B/2/P